Death, Desire, and Other Destinations

Death, Desire, and Other Destinations

Stories

By Tara Isabel Zambrano

Okay Donkey Press

Published by Okay Donkey Press

Los Angeles, CA 90034

www.okaydonkeymag.com

First Edition. September 2020.

ISBN: 978-1-7332441-4-5

Cover art: Sarah E. Shields

TABLE OF CONTENTS

Alligators

The stare of the tribal girl, taut as a cable. She sits opposite to me, next to an older woman, probably her mother, in an open truck. Because of the bus drivers' strike, I have hitched a ride from Jaipur to Jaisalmer. The girl's tattoos shine in the air, purple ink on sunburned skin, a small nose, a slight overbite. I don't know if she's looking at me or past me. The wind is making puffy noises in our ears, pouring the desert. The tire marks follow us until we are on a tar road. The truck jerks and the girl lets out a sharp cry. She has thin lips. It's hard to imagine the piercing sound that came from her throat. The early morning light coats my eyes.

When my mother committed suicide, I was ten, and at the time was playing in my room with a Barbie she got for my birthday. My father did not cry. He adjusted his spectacles, called her a hungry shadow, and carried on with his life. Some relatives claimed my mother often talked about a sacred river where spirits slept, a forest where every tree was an animal in its previous life. She drew illustrations of foxes and snakes with human faces, and about how we borrowed bodies and faces from hell and heaven, demons and saints.

We pass by small tea stalls and repair shops, the bicyclists who prefer to ride off-road, shouting crudest insults. A sparrow sits on the side of the truck, just a strange rush of wind between us. I look at the tribal girl, a slight reflection of light at the edge of her face. I can smell her sweat and a warm, serpentine feeling takes root in my gut and grows. The sight of her eyes makes me want. Maybe she's thinking magic between her sun-squinted eyes, while she continues to twist the edge of her dupatta around her finger.

I'm wearing my mother's kurta. I'm carrying her dresses, her scarves, her socks in my backpack. Her kajal. I am carrying her ashes. Before her demise, I didn't know how much space a life required: beyond a room, beyond a house, beyond a glance or a touch, the whole world. Now I know how much space the dead need.

There is a dead baby alligator blocking the road. The truck stops and we all get down wondering how it got there. The old woman asks us to pick it up. Her voice has an authority none of us can challenge. Her arms are covered with thick silver bangles and her fingers are filled with rings. On her forehead: a tattoo of a snake eating its tail. She says it's a bad omen if we leave the animal behind. Her words cut through the air. It will bring a long-drawn illness on all of us, a shame, a curse, she adds and stares at the horizon. The driver lifts the beast and wedges it between the rows of passengers, its thick armor weighing the air down. It smells like sewage and burnt rubber.

The girl looks at me, licks her lips, her eyes pink with dust and exhaust. I clear my throat and tie my hair up in a bun. The day's heat burns at my nape. Between us, an occasional breeze, the rattling doors of the truck, rings of sweat in my armpits. I am holding the rail on the edge, its metal hot in my hand. We pass the railway crossing, and the kids playing near the railway tracks yell and whistle. The boys on the truck shout back. The girl raises her face towards the big, silver sky at this hour, closes her eyes and lets the sunlight soak her face. The truck rises and sinks over the tracks on the ground. Rubbing against our feet like coarse sugar, the animal's body wobbles, blood and slime out of its mouth pooling in the corners as the vehicle steers into the dissolving light and the keen euphoria of birds at this hour.

I must have been about twelve when I started locking my bedroom door at night and in the morning, would find it unlatched. Unable to sleep for days, weeks, I sat by the window, suspecting my mother would enter my room any moment. But nothing ever happened. Perhaps my mother was watching me while I was awake, and only left the room when I fell asleep.

The tribal girl follows me to the bathroom and in a dark corner pulls out a cigarette and lights a match. The burning butt looks like a red laser dot. To extinguish the match, she runs her tongue over it. Then she hands me the cigarette and asks me to keep the heat in a bit longer before letting the smoke out. It keeps the warmth in your words, she says. Her voice sticks to my skin, our outlines coalesced in vapor. She caresses the fabric of my kurta, smells it and lifts it. Prickles of dry skin grow wet. Her gaze cleaves me open. She unbuttons my jeans, pushes her fingers down, the cold surfaces of her rings maneuver inside my body, one by one. The sun is long gone. The weight of her one hand rests on my waist, the reek of urine in the air, makes me squirm. I push her against the wall, and we are a tangle of tongues. A lone bulb with sickly yellow light shines on the other side of the bathroom. Her tattoos rise and fall with every breath, until I let out a muffled moan and it seems her eyes move all the way up to where her head begins. Slick everywhere, I blink. They return to where they are meant to be.

I stay in the same spot after the girl withdraws. The space between us thickens as she licks her fingers.

Afterwards, she tells me that the old woman is not her mother.

Walking back to the truck, I feel heavy and out of breath, as if I'm climbing a hill.

I needed someone to pull out my nightmares, the tribal girl says.

Nightmares?

I see dead alligators in my dreams, she whispers and runs her bronze, still-wet finger on my lips.

In the distance, Jaisalmer looks monstrous, with its twinkling incandescent eyes.

I recall the gloomy bedrooms: my mother on the bed, a black scarf tied around her head, dad sleeping on his solitary bed in a separate room. In the morning, he wouldn't look at her or talk to her and she'd hover around him like a ghost begging for life. Later, unable to say anything, I'd oil and braid her hair and the rose tattoo on the back of her neck would deepen in color with every breath of mine.

The alligator has started to rot. Its suffocating odor pervades the air. The tribal mother urges us to carry it a little longer. The girl sits next to me, our thighs rubbing, our nostrils burnt under a common stench. The boys on the opposite row are staring at us. The wind brushes her long locks on my face. For one fleeting moment, I want to tell her that she's beautiful, but she doesn't need to be told that. There's no before or after for her. She knows who she is; she hasn't curled up after sex, like I have.

I open the backpack: it's all in there, the clothes, the kajal, and the ashes. Her smell. I wonder if there's a way for someone to pull out the loss from me.

The tribal girl holds my hand: her rough, scaly skin lunges and lurks under the passing streetlamps, a sensation like rolling marbles up and down my spine. The old woman pushes the beads of a rosary, her eyes roll back, her lips mumble. She says something to the girl and the girl responds with a nod. The air gets a few degrees colder. Suddenly weary, I place my head on her shoulder, a dark muscled trunk.

I dream that my father and the old woman from the truck are rubbing my mother's body raw with turmeric and sandalwood until all that is left is sand, a desert. Then they open my legs and empty it inside me. My chest is prickly, a cactus filled with sap. An alligator grows in my womb. When it's born, it devours me whole.

I wake up and we're crossing a river, its water dark as oil, my teeth dug into the tribal girl's shoulders, a sharp, metallic taste of blood filling my mouth, unspooling warmth in my breath. We're passing by streetlights, thin florescent tubes electric above us, the sky dark, expanding with quiet. The girl pats my face, asks me to go back to sleep. The boys are snoring and drooling, they whisper indecipherable phrases like prophecies. Far away, dogs howl, a pack of hyenas scream.

The moon is swallowed behind a row of clouds. When it emerges like a half-illuminated hip, the tribal mother lets out a wail, says it is time for them to get down. The driver asks her if we can get rid of the alligator. She shrugs her shoulders as the girl helps her down. Two boys pick up the animal and throw it by the roadside. Under a faint streetlight, the beast looks like a mound of dirt. Finite, done. The girl and the old woman walk into the night, the jingle of their ornaments audible for a bit, then lost. Abandoned, I hold on to the shape her body has left behind in me, part home, part grave. The engine revs and I turn around to a sound. The alligator shudders, its bulging eyes shining near the edge of its head. I let out a cry and keep looking at it, blinking. Until it goes back to being dead. Until it disappears into the night.

Lunar Love

We fly to the moon to exchange our vows. Karen and Mia, our suits say with little red hearts next to them. On earth, for the past year, we have wrestled with this idea to go to the moon, we have argued about the endless waitlist, the long travel and spending all our savings. We have been excited about doing something that everyone we know does these days since they find nothing exciting about the earth anymore. We have spent sleepless nights after practicing in reduced gravity chambers, stayed in our PJs and pigtails for days, thinking of endless space, soaking up the light. We have broken up thrice and made up, the moon waxing and waning in the background, its simplicity, its grandeur, pulling us in like tides.

The wedding-on-moon event planner warns us that there will be no holding hands or kissing the bride, there will be no flowers. Only words that we can carve on the moon rocks we bring back. We are ready to be startled by the void, the cramped spaceship, to be together on something so far removed from remembering to put the trashcans out on Wednesdays, hating neighbors who didn't approve of us as a couple, alternating between CBD and Melatonin, waiting for IVF to work. We touch our bellies, try to imagine the weightlessness in our bones. Will the days feel fluffy? Will we sync up on our cycles? The planner makes us sign a hundred-page contract in case mission control loses contact with the spaceship. If we are gone, kidnapped by the space.

We land on the moon and the barren grey shell overcomes us, as if it has done something irreparably wrong. We click a selfie next to a sore crater. We hum our favorite songs. *I do.* Our helmets touch. We whisper our promises. Your eyes catch mine. *I do.* You pick up some dust, I collect some rocks. *'Till death do us part.* No, not that, something else. The silence grows on us. This seems like a wonderland, all ours. No neighbors. Until, at a distance, another ship lands. White dots on a blank canvas. A vast ocean of darkness ahead, as if we are kids on a beach, up late on a new moon night.

We bounce around, you make a cartoon face. I giggle. I push you slightly, want to feel your warmth again. I want to ask you, when will I be able to take you to that famous hotdog joint at the edge of our town, and pretend to read your palm and get you all excited? I want to tell you we'll stay married no matter what. I'll make dinner for you and you'll do our laundry. We'll get pregnant one day. You point in a direction, as if you saw something. Perhaps a star, it's light reaching us long after it has burned out. For a few minutes, I follow but see nothing. You are still looking, your head tilted right like you do when you are focused or pushing your tongue inside my mouth, and I recall our first kiss, my fingers in your curly hair, electric from the contact. Later that afternoon, at my place, our skins stitched together, my lips on your left breast. Your face glowing as if lit with a kilowatt bulb. My slick fingers dug between your legs, then a pink explosion, a small wet moon glistening on the sheet, quickly disappearing. Afterwards, the dim light flickering on our toes like Morse code, a hint of love. A room of lavender, yellow, aching red.

I lean in, but you have moved away, and I see your insulated boots leaving giant footprints that don't look like they belong to your shapely feet.

You have reached the crater. The white of your suit blurs along the edges. I can't make out anything clearly. The absence of color fills the space between us: fluid, thick, hard to cut through. I miss the sun.

On our way back, there is no language. I look for signs, imaginary orbits that keep the planets latched in, the gravity that snaps our hearts below our heads. There is only clean black, a rattling vibration and smooth slipping of needles in their gauges. Everything as planned. I make a mental list of to-do things when we return: mow the overgrown grass, erase all the pictures and research on the moon from our phones, scan the sperm donor files once again—11320 is a football player, 17216 is a Harvard graduate, 21412 is a painter. I turn towards you and you are staring at me, your hand on my thigh like you do when you're about to fall asleep and we are shooting down like a comet, homebound, light creases on our cheeks, catching a glimpse of each other's eyes.

Wherever, Whenever

Baba bought a Christmas tree because Tania insisted on it. Two weeks later, at circle time, everyone in her class is going to talk about unwrapping gifts around a Christmas tree. And she does not want to be left out just because we don't go to church on Sundays; we worship several Gods and Goddesses in a temple, adorned by flowers, covered in sandalwood fragrance, called on by constant ringing of bells.

Ma sits quietly in the kitchen, stares at the mottled bark of oak in the backyard, her face a roiling ocean of emotions, her neck perpetually taut. She gets up and stirs the gravy for mutton, whispers to herself. Outside, the sunlight is shallow. Soon the festive mayhem will be over. It's hard to explain to our friends and their parents why we don't celebrate Christmas, and watch their faces drop. _Hindus, you said?_ They ask, _Like Buddhists?_

At the dinner table we say our prayers. Tania and I don't close our eyes. We watch our parents, their heads bowed, and hands folded, whispering shlokas from ancient Hindu text. Unlike

American parents, Ma and Baba don't touch each other in public. Ma never wears pants or skirts even though she has remarkable legs.

Ma instructs me to close my mouth while chewing. Tania asks about the ornaments for the Christmas tree. Ma suggests using her imitation earrings, old necklaces, and silk handkerchiefs. Tania shrugs, I know she's disappointed. We talk about decorating the house and Pa says we can use the oil lamps from Diwali. *It's not the same,* Tania resists. From the overhead bulb, light splashes on her face. She urges Ma and Baba to buy a few strings of bulbs for the tree in the front yard, sweating through her fleece. I place my hand over hers. Ma continues to suck the bone, little lumps of marrow falling on her plate, her fingers licked clean.

After the dinner, I pull out the trash cans to the roadside. The air pokes everywhere, a chill spreading through my body faster than fire. The houses are decorated like brides. I collect the mail and stay in the driveway listening to the distant evening traffic. I don't feel I belong here, not in the way Ma and Baba talk about their village in India, how they made it out to America for a better life for them and their kids. I don't think I belong where they come from. I am only familiar with a few alphabets of Hindi, garam masala and turmeric, differentiation between a few Hindu castes based on their last names. Tania and I are at the border: our citizenship is a string of digits in our passport, our ethnicity a questionnaire our parents wish we knew the answers to. We can

look on either side and not find a home. Between my dusky
fingers, flyers flap: coupons for clothes and jewelry, symmetrical
trees that go up to the ceiling.

Our fake tree stands next to the fireplace we never use and
clean once a year. The LEDs blink hard: yellow and red. *Isn't it
nice?* Baba says, lounging in his easy chair, smiling, extending his
right arm towards me. Yes, I nod my head and hand him the mail,
wishing I was like him: feeling at ease, wherever, whenever. He
has never said *I love you* to any of us. The words just don't come.
In the background, the vents vibrate like small-winged birds, blast
warm, dry air and he asks me to reduce the temperature. Then he
goes back to reading the mail and the room glows in an artificial
light, like a town in the middle of nowhere.

[handwritten notes in top margin: mother's new boyfriend feels up daughter beside mother cooking]

Up and Up

[handwritten: Gross]

Six months after my dad's death, when I visit my mother, the front door is unlocked. In the bedroom, my mother is covered in moans; a stranger's head between her legs. She notices me as I gasp and walk away; sit in the living room, my mouth dry and my hands between my thighs.

What was that, I bawl, when she comes out, tying her robe, her nipples visible through the satin, her Indian brown eyes bold and bright.

This is Santosh, my mother says and the stranger steps aside from behind her. He's wearing checkered boxers and a white cotton vest. Thin lips and a butt chin, a full head of curly hair. My dad was bald and wore dentures.

My mother starts preparing lamb pulao, my favorite. She asks Santosh to get a few ripe mangoes from the tree in our backyard. I'm pacing between the patio and the living room, occasionally glancing at my dad's picture hanging on the side wall, adorned by a garland, his eyes staring ahead as if he chooses

[handwritten: set]

to ignore it. Outside the peonies in the garden sway in a light breeze. White, burgundy, and pink. When I walk back into the kitchen, my mother is rinsing the meat, a lace of fat on her finger pads, a scent of dad's aftershave emanating from her body.

He's probably half your age, I say, my voice filled with contempt. *Mmm hmm*, she answers and tosses the chops in a turmeric-paprika-yogurt mix.

Would you like some raita with rice? She looks at me, her gaze rich with profundity, defiance. She looks beautiful.

I grab her arm. My eyes are wet, my lips trembling.

You should be scared; he might run away with all your belongings. Worse, he might kill you. What do our neighbors think, what about dad?

My mother breaks into a laugh and signals vaguely at the air. *It's a blessing to be alive with no one to answer to*, she says.

Santosh arrives from the back door in the kitchen, holding three mangoes. He places them in a line on the concrete platform, next to the sink, and stands behind me. I feel his breath on the small of my back, a low call, my pores opening onto wonder, previous half-baked climaxes and affairs slipping out, my body poured into a new cast. He tongues my ear while my mother hums an old song and drains the soaked basmati rice—the moisture stuffed grains stuck to each other, soft. She looks at me, her face exuding light as if asking me to go on. Then she turns around to start the stove. Santosh places his hands on my blouse, the heat of his skin warming my breasts. His eyes are smooth as sea glass, beckoning.

I place his hand below my navel and his fingers slip down. From the corner of my eye, I see my mother squeezing mangoes, her palms smeared in pulp. She licks them clean. In the background, the pressure cooker hisses until it can no longer hold the smell of the melting flesh, the steam rising, up and up, dispersing, until we are slick with it.

Milk

We latch on to our mother's breasts even after we're grownups. Her nipples look like worn hooks attached to a swollen wall. There isn't much inside, but we like the closeness, and the clicking sound, her topless body attached to our hungry mouths. Her breasts blossom in summer, her body bounces like a stuffed toy. In winter she is vacuous and frumpy.

When the milk does not trickle for several days, we go out and bring a baby barely breathing we found by the dumpster. Mother looks at him and cries, brings him up close, the nipple too big for his tiny mouth. The baby's body curls like a kidney bean when he latches on, his tiny fists pressing against mother's skin. Mother laughs, she doesn't look like our mother anymore. The baby falls asleep in her arms, a part of her breast pressed against his cheek. We run outside, push our toes in dirt and circle the yard several times, wondering if it was a good idea to bring the baby.

There are no rules for the baby. Mother says that's because the baby is damaged, that he needs strength. So, the next day and the day after, and for many days, the baby latches on to her, holds and pulls her hair as the clicking sound hits our ears and turns our heads. Mother hums and smiles, showers twice a day, starts braiding her hair. She sews onesies from the cloth she got for our shirts, puts his handprints in a scrapbook while we scrub the floor, wash the sheets, bring our mouths close to her body and plead for her milk.

One day when she is cleaning the yard, we grab the baby and put him next to the dumpster where we found him, the stack of onesies next to his smooth, kicking legs. When we get back, mother is holding a stick, her body soaking up all the light, her mouth a hole filled with curses. She hisses and pulls our hair, shoves us. We tell her we don't know where the baby is while the stick hits us behind the knees, on the back and the arms, forming a litter of blisters. Her breasts bounce making us believe we did the right thing. Tired, she squats in our tall shadows and looks out the window as if she no longer sees us. Then she exclaims how perfectly whole the baby was, how rich the smell of his spit, how soft his mouth on her nipples. And suddenly, we realize our mother will always love the baby because he had no teeth, because he could not dig into her body and break her heart.

Scooped-Out Chest

When I slice a knife down my chest, my heart crawls out. It looks healthy, full. Cherry red inside out. I watch it drag itself on the floor, onto my desk overlooking the yard and the trees. Blood drips from its sides. Outside, the moon floats on the cloudy horizon, fuzzy on the perimeter.

In front of the mirror, my heart mouths words. It complains I haven't been an optimistic person, I don't drink enough water, I always wear black. When I read a joke circulated on WhatsApp, my heart laughs, it has teeth, sharp fat deposits. We talk about the boys I liked, the towns I lived in and hated, the men I slept with and said I love you to with different levels of uncertainty. I offer bourbon and the heart gulps down in one go, the knots of blood growing darker.

My heart and I go grocery shopping and fill our cart with chocolate ice cream and potato chips. At home, the TV gleams in the background: arguing couples on Fixer Upper, pretending to be excited. In its gentle cautious voice, my heart whispers my secrets into the night, a large chip stuck to its side like a tongue. *Shh,* I say, and one by one the indiscretions rise like smoke, hover as if holding us hostage and then merge into the white of the ceiling. The heart puffs up like a windsock with all the space released inside it. I watch it earnestly: if this is the way it's supposed to be, but almost never is.

In the middle of the night, the heart curled up next to me like a lover, confesses that it's impossible for it to go back in my body and beat endlessly, needlessly. I watch its surface: smoothed and rounded by time and ache, a muscle flexing, stroking, concentrating on a thought.

What should I do with this? I point to my scooped-out chest: a fleshless hole, a peculiar sickness settling in my gut. The heart brushes itself on my cheek, its salty smell goes up my nose.

Oh shit, I murmur, feeling cold as a coin, shivering. *I'm sorry to let you* down, I say. My throat stings, I drank too much whiskey.

It's okay, it whispers and places its mouth between my legs. I see a bridge of capillaries, the atria and ventricles soaked in milky blood drinking my fire. Then it jumps down from the bed and tows itself away, a thin trail of ice cream behind it. I wonder if I'll die in a moment, an hour or never, if my heart ever belonged to me.

We have always found our way back to each other, I shout. A door opens and closes. I put my ear to the ground, hear the thumping growing weaker, and imagine all my blood and sins leaving their sliver of a stomach. *Still here?* I ask in a voice that doesn't sound like mine, a voice dragged out of a body that's learning what it feels like to be left behind.

Spaceman

I used to be an astronaut, he says, seated next to me in a downtown bar, sipping beer. I turn my head towards him. I am dressed in black tights and a red cardigan, thick, black curls and a heavy mascara. He is tall, his face lost to poor lighting. I eye his hands, trimmed nails and wrinkled knuckles. He reminds me of you minus the tattoo on his forearm.

He offers the next round of drinks. I am not so sure, but I go along. *So how does it feel to be in space,* I ask. He taps the wooden floor with his shoes.

It's like mixing with the night, the darkness numbs the image of colors in your head, he answers. *The gravity tricks your body about what it has known all along.*

That's poetic.

Yes, he says and gulps the rest of his beer. *That's what it is, space is poetic.* He places his hand next to mine, the edge of our pinkies touching.

I buried my husband a month ago, I say. *I shouldn't be here.*

*

Outside, on the sidewalk, he follows me. *Listen,* he calls out and grabs my arm. His hand is warm, firm. His eyes are sad, compassionate. We kiss, wander towards a deserted parking lot, the thin ribs of fluorescent light above us, flickering. I hear his zipper, my fingers in his wild hair, my tongue swirling in the dark of his mouth, numbing my senses, disappearing. Then he withdraws and says he wants to take me home.

How far? I ask, a rush of nerves overwhelming me.

Around the block. He points to a high rise.

When we pass by a restaurant, I see couples kissing, swaying to light jazz. I have never seen this side of night when you were around. We always slept early, got up early. Yoga, meditation retreats. Understanding the way to live, to die. Now, here on the sidewalk, is a world I haven't witnessed in a long time. It's careless, alive. For a moment, I imagine what would you say? He pulls me close. I slightly bite his ear, unknowingly. His head is leaned in, a light chill settling on my exposed cheek.

*

His apartment is filled with piles of books, posters on the walls, the surface of moon, craters. A heap of clothes on the side. He presses his face against my chest. I interlace my fingers with his. Soft, yielding. Suddenly, he lifts his head. *Did you love him, your husband?* I avoid his eyes, glance at a dark corner. I make a mental list of all the things I've left behind: my wedding ring, my pager, my phone, my sense of urgency to get back to you. I'm supposed to be still in love with you but I'm here. He plays with my curls. *I've been in love,* he says. *It felt as if I was in a reduced gravity chamber, my insides tumbling.* I laugh. *Never heard that before.* The lightness in my voice surprises me.

*

My tights and cardigan are off, he is in his boxers: little rockets with blazing trails. The bed is small for both of us. *I've become used to being in cramped spaces,* he says. The rain gently taps at the windows. He kisses my bare breasts, licks my navel, my clit. The apartment feels like a boat without oars. He digs his tongue deep, until I am spent, until I can't move anymore.

*

I don't tell him that you and I slept in separate beds. I don't tell him that in the past few years I cared for you like a mother takes care of her child. How you moved from our bedroom to the couch and then the hospital bed. Hours ache by as I dream about being lost in darkness, my body spinning in space, naked.

When I wake up, I hear the breaking of shells, possibly eggs crackling as they hit the hot oil. I feel hungry and sad. *What am I doing?* I push my curls behind my ears, I put on my clothes. I am ready to leave when he holds my hand, squeezes it.

Come, eat with me, he says. *Stay.* He's smiling. White teeth, eyes squeezing up.

For a moment, he sounds like you, luring me, showing me, this is the life I need, this *is* the life. In the meantime, the rain keeps coming down, a satisfying sickness in my stomach, as if it's filled with fog. I'm thinking of you, your gentle, cautious voice, *Stay*. A clink, a swish. We're flying in darkness, the air cooler, a strong fishy smell. We're escaping gravity, my insides tumbling. A kiss. I'm moving my tongue. I'm ready to climb again. Your hands moving to my waist. *Stay.* Then lower, lower, lower.

Piecing

You're about to slip into your creased loafers.

"Wait," I say and put the thermometer away, prop pillows.

The navy tie rubs between my breasts. The steam from the nonstick iron hisses. You forgot to turn it off.

"Fuck," you whisper.

*

I dream of all the mothers I know. They're laughing, saying something too soft for me to hear. Their children are playing on the beach, their soft bottoms covered in sand and water, too precious to touch.

*

In the storeroom, there are unopened boxes with photo albums, old letters. There's a notebook of your ghazals. I run my fingers over the blue velvet cover. It's as soft as the lyrics inside. I pull out a clock. Hands stuck at 6:30—time blooming between the instant when the clock froze and now. A move from Mumbai to Delhi because of your promotion. The doctors visits, fucking, squirrels going up and down the trees, street dogs napping in slow mornings, spiderwebs on forgotten corners, shimmering. Fucking. Waiting. Honks trilling on both sides of the roads. Both of us conscious of every passing hour, making our way back to each other at the end of every day.

*

The next time you enter me, I start piecing a baby together. Cells building up on top of each other—a circus tent, taut, blistering. A few weeks later it collapses as if the stakes are pulled from the ground. For the rest of the week, I hunt jobs on the internet, create career profiles, Google search "miscarriages," again.

*

At the restaurant, you order fried fish, sip your red wine, and look around.

"Had a good day?"

I nod and go back to the menu. From my gut, something rises to my throat. It's 7:00 p.m., and I wonder if this is what morning sickness feels like.

Outside, clouds gargle and spit a few drops. A Bollywood song frolics through the static of an old radio in a roadside shack. I take your arm and watch my feet quickly moving in front of me.

*

Over the weekend, we visit Qutub Minar, a tall, tapering tower five stories high. In Arabic, it means "pole" or "axis." It has a spiral staircase of 379 steps. At the foot of the tower is the first mosque built in India. An inscription over its eastern gate states that it was built with material obtained from demolishing twenty-seven Hindu temples.

You shake your head in disapproval. A tour guide starts walking with us, his eyes big and brown, hair long and girlish.

"The structure leans a little due to a lot of construction and deconstruction in the past," he says in a mix of Hindi and English.

*

The tour guide takes us to a seven-meter-high iron pillar standing in the courtyard of the mosque. It's two thousand years old and hasn't rusted. "If you can encircle it with your hands while standing with your back to it," he claims, "your wish will be fulfilled."

We try several times. On our way back, we don't speak, only listen to the hum of the car's engine. The humidity makes our eyes water.

*

At home, I unpack the iron wok, refill the spices, knead dough for naan. You check the latest score of a cricket match on the tube. My hands, deep in the mix of flour and yeast, make a mound—a body ready to rise. I want to remind you about the doctor's appointment day after tomorrow. I want to discuss adoption. But you're thrilled to find out that the Indian skipper scored another half-century just off thirty-five balls.

*

I'm in the bathroom, on my knees, stinking wet, scrubbing the floor—trying to get the bloodstains out. I'm trying not to think of your tongue circling around my navel, reaching lower, my hips squirming. I'm trying not to cry.

*

When the monsoon takes a break, we're out in the city from early afternoon until the sun drops behind the skyscrapers. India Gate and Red Fort. Jama Masjid. Sampling spices and silver jewelry in Chandni Chowk, hustling in the crowded, narrow streets. At home, we kick our shoes off and lean on the couch. Around us the walls look sickly, faded, the floor is the color of aged mulch. You say, "We need to paint these walls. Lavender, cherry blossom pink, or baby blue."

*

I dream my baby is born in pieces, head, torso, limbs—all separate. I stitch him with a black thread so I can see the seams. His teeth are sharp and too many, spilling from his mouth. My breasts are sore, engorged, filled with blood. Once while changing him, I accidentally pull the string, and he comes undone.

*

My sister calls when you're out for a run. "Any news?" she asks. "Usual," I say and chuckle nervously. She talks about different treatments, while I tiptoe down the hall and step outside. The sky is the shade of water. On the sidewalk, a toddler boy turns his torso towards me, a neon-orange bib on his chest, a string of saliva between his mouth and neck, his cheeks pink. We make eye contact. "Yes, I've heard of acupuncture," I hear myself answer.

*

I start the washer, sit in the bathtub, and think about the city. Beauty from destruction. Destruction of beauty. Nothing is safe, not even a belief.

Before the water drains, I stand up and glance at myself in the full-length mirror. Like Qutub, I lean on one side.

*

Outside, the rain falls loose like coins from a hole in the pocket. I inspect and fold all the washed clothes—no stains, only faint outlines.

*

Your face is peaceful, dipped in dreams. I bring your notebook to bed. The perfect handwriting makes me weep.

Turn my head at every sound, not so much now.

Regret takes refuge in me, not so much now.

Was her hair brown? Her face an autumn evening?

I remember she was me, not so much now.

Heart-shaped envelopes, a book of ghazal, stuffed with songs and starlit sleep, not so much now.

From the border, the bullets travel in dust—leave your wounded memories, not so much now.

One night of full moon, your arm around my waist, it's all I wanted to see, not so much now.

On your grave, flowers stoop like old, cold widows.

Light was taxing, rain came free, not so much now.

The wind beats its chest against the door.

It awaits your scent to leave, not so much now.

*

Almost midnight. I can still smell your aftershave—it's that time of the month again. All my nerve endings are alive. Naked, I sneak over to you, ecstasy braided in my spine. Between your legs my simmering lips build you up like a rain cloud. Half-awake, you take me in your arms, splashing my insides white. I stay still with my hands on my belly, your light snores slipping into my ears, the armor of my body against yours, our little tremors sounding like far-off explosions in another century. Bloodshed, rubble. A new monument rising from the ruins. And in the darkness, I smile, thinking how much that light quaking resembles a baby's footsteps.

hyp[i]cropsy of
muslim faith

Silent Spaces

The girl in the hijab, a high schooler, is eager to caress her best friend's thighs, bite her broad back that tapers into a thin waist. She packs vegetable sandwiches and honey mustard pretzels for her date with Rebekah. "I'll be back before the evening prayer," she says and kisses her mother on both cheeks. The sky is the color of faded denim. A haze of heat, a steel glaze, flowers swaying in shimmering breeze like ballerinas.

At the beach house, Rebekah stands naked under a butter-colored penlight, a tattoo of a snake biting its tail bold and bright on her wrist. The girl in the hijab traces eight with her fingers on her friend's breasts. She then licks Rebekah's navel—It blooms, and her head is filled with a sweet lavender scent, her nose flaming rouge. Outside the palm leaves stir like wings of a bird.

Rebekah removes the hijab, runs her tongue on the girl's earlobe. She unhooks the kurta, pushes the jeans down her ankles, her fingers flitting purposely between the girl's dusky legs letting out a secret odor.

Muslims

"Look at me," Rebekah instructs, and from the edges of her eyes, the girl sees her friend fuzzy—clouds hovering over her body, ready to give, until it's all a collage of a sound and a shudder, a pink stain on the marble floor.

In the shower, Rebekah shaves the girl's legs, her underarms, the crimpy bush. The sweeping hair crescents look like an Arabic script. She lowers her head onto the girl's nipples. They smell of rosewater and sandalwood, button hard. A reminder buzzes on the girl's phone. Rebekah shakes the towel.

"Do you have to pray now?"

"Not really," the girl responds and tries on Rebekah's orange two-piece swimsuit, astonished to see how her loose and shrouded body fits into something so skimpy. Rebekah adjusts the bra straps and the cups, combs the girl's tangled hair—the wind in her curls.

The beach is a glaring mirror. The girl talks about the way her father moans with a rosary, her mother stone-faced and quiet, watching soaps on TV all day long, her brothers, skinny boys dreaming of manhood and finally the man, who goes to the same mosque her family does, groping and trying to kiss her.

Rebekah chews on the sandwiches, sips her Coke. "My parents are rarely at home. Some days, lying on my bed when I'm touching myself, I hear the bunnies and the squirrels rustling through the low leaves in the garden, burrowing. A stray cat roaming around, meowing. When I get up to see them, they're only shadows."

"We should go on a vacation," the girl says and stares at the white foam of the sea, imagining their folded clothes on top of each other in the same suitcase, their bodies on a motel bed like tangled necklaces in a jewelry box.

"Where?"

"A nowhere town," the girl sings touching her bare legs— the open pores soaking the sun and the possibilities.

The girl watches Rebekah rising and falling with the waves, lapping into them like an old lover. "Teach me how to swim, pleeease!" she shouts, squinting her eyes.

In shoulder-deep water, Rebekah lines her head and toes. Then she comes up, swipes her hands over her wet hair, specks of salt shining on her neck. "The body's designed to float," she says, pushing her toes into the wet sand.

"If that were true why would anyone drown?"

Rebekah shrugs, "because they don't know how to let go."

The evening falls on its knees. The girl ties her hair, puts on her hijab. She kisses Rebekah, whispers in her ears. Behind the roof of the beach house, the girl in the hijab notices the purple goodbye of the day, the silent spaces between the chirps. Her father has spoken of resisting the temptations, his endless ranting—*don't smoke, don't drink, no sex*—murmuring the rewards in the afterlife. She walks past a long row of birds on the wire over the red light just as it changes, and they rise one by one, perfectly timed. She knows what she'll do after the prayer, after the dinner has been cleared away, after she's alone—the dark of her eyes glinting on the windowpanes licked by noisy bugs, her body floating in the air spilling moonlight, blowing away close.

loss of faith? (handwritten)

the shrinking circle

I am unable to close my eyes. God is sitting in front of me. He turns around and stares into a pit on the internet that is downloading a new game. His watch, a radium-green, showcases his elephantine toothed smile. I try to sleep while He starts digging graves. I help Him and we do not take any breaks. The next morning, I pass out in History class.

poetry (handwritten)

*

I latch to a new earth, magical stories written on the sky. There are only words and dust in my pocket. Time wrapped around my chest like a bomb. My skin is nothing but dirt, tied to the land. I am told I will die one day, alone and helpless.

*

I start working in a Mexican takeout. While I fill the burritos with tomatoes, meat and sweat, I think of a girl in my Statistics class, the one with azure eyes and the smell of tangerine lingering on her fingertips. I wish to quit my instinct and kiss her.

perversion of god (handwritten)

After work, I wait for her and follow her to an abandoned shed where she fucks a bald guy with tattoos all over his arms.

*

I am fired, because of my midnight quesadilla cravings. At home, I microwave ham and cheese. The appliance groans as if I am cooking a storm. I raise the blinds and decide never to have kids. I want to join a circus. When I turn to get my food, I see God's feet tapping outside the door. Morse code. S-O-S. My feet screwed to the vinyl floor, my pockets inside out, I feel the tongue of death swiping over my thoughts every time the microwave beeps. It is starting to smell like rain.

*

God is inside the room with me. We play the game on my computer. Then I sit next to Him and start massaging His feet. He places His mouth on mine. His breath is doused in tangerine and there is fresh ink blotched on His swollen arms. My heart fried black, sits inside the microwave, getting cold. But I continue to massage. And all we do is glare at each other, around the shrinking circle of His watch.

Girl Loss

At night, dead girls roam in the neighborhood. It's the middle of January and the roads are sprinkled with salt, lined with single-story shacks with missing shingles and cheap sidings. They didn't know each other before they died. Now they sit on the cul-de-sac and share a smoke. The air around them turns gray.

Sometimes, Chelsea finds herself at the base of the lake. Black, ripped tights and a red tank top, the sound in her throat like sloshing water in a jug. Josey, her boyfriend, still swipes through her naked pictures on his phone, her never-trimmed hair covering her breasts, touching her pubes. Pouting lips, watery-blue eyes and her stubborn paleness fading into the background. In the mornings, he jogs past her house and imagines her silhouette behind broken blinds, removing her night retainer, later picking at her scalp while struggling with her calculus homework. Or in the back of his pickup, in her dollar-store lingerie and pumps, holding his head—feeling the tip of his tongue in her throat. Or lying face turned sideways on a floater in the lake without the fear of drowning.

Dried blood extends from Lata's left eyebrow to her thin shoulder blade, a dark, deep wound above her left ear. She sits with her weight shifted on the right hip as if leaning against the night. Ten houses away, her auto mechanic father microwaves soy nuggets and eats them in front of the TV, his large knuckled hands resting in the empty bowl like they used to between Lata's legs, his sweat and grease suffocating her, staining the sheets and her panties. Every Tuesday and Thursday, he wanders around the only temple in the town and makes donations in hope of seeking redemption, cries in the prayer meetings as he rolls up the sleeves of his white kurta. The images in his head keep playing non-stop—the shaking bed and fear-paled Lata staring into the ceiling, her body a rainbow of bruises, shivering.

The needle marks on Sian's hands have healed but the hallucinations continue. Each vein in her body felt like a sparkler. She became lost in the rapture of daydreams that made her fuck dealers. She often passed out in her bed and woke up with her thin, crack-numbed limbs, a forest of visible nerves underneath the skin ready to burst.

The girls don't talk about how they died. They untangle each other's locks, the insides of their mouths still pink, their eyes sparkling with mist. They rope their arms around each other's waists, shush gently about going to a beach—feel the hot sand on their chilled and aching bodies, gaze at the sunlight ground into a moonstone. Before the dawn foams and softens the purple-edged horizon, they see Venus low in the sky; realize they haven't survived up to their eighteenth birthday. The treetops turn from dark grey to peach, the roofs of the houses they lived in, visible, their sharp edges up. Fidgety in their skin, they conclude they've died without living. They're still dying. They call out their names, watch the dust bury their words in the hungry earth. Then they cross their arms above their chests to feel something move but their hearts remain. Still, very still.

In Its Entire Splendor

My lover is big, as dense as a neutron star, his eyes two cosmic lenses. When he licks my collar bone, his words roll off his tongue and settle around my neck like a choker.

"Are you ready for the roller coaster, Sweetie?" he whispers, shaking the ground, before he angles my shoulders and swallows me, his mouth opened wide, a row of white, jagged peaks, a quivering, slippery wormhole ahead.

It's for my benefit, he claims. All his ex-lovers are inside him, away from diseases and predators. I duck my head and let go. Past the carotid artery and trachea, I hold on to one of the ribs and stick my legs in. It almost feels like we are doing a 69 as I linger in the headstand position rubbing against his lungs, my aorta flickering as his, in its entire splendor.

I slip into the stomach and find the leftovers of his past lovers. Some couldn't sustain the swallowing; others were not in harmony with his body. I can tell he tried to stitch some of them, but it was too late. And despite the muck and bile, it's all beautiful:

a shrine of love and hope that makes his blood more vibrant, his breath sweet, reminiscent of all. His body is a supernova where I am safe and warm.

His larynx flutters; it's my favorite song. "Can you hear it, Sweetie?" he yells. I push my fist against his muscular abdomen. He laughs. I know what he's thinking. No more compromises or conflicts, only true, unified love, opening and closing forever like the valves of his heart.

He says I am the strongest. I have a chance.

The Moons of Jupiter

When Ramirez starts moving inside me, I know I'll be blind for the rest of the day. Something unstable with my optic nerves or, as Dr. Santoor described it to me, transient bitemporal visual loss as a physiological response to sexual activity. And I sat in his office staring at his raised eyebrows, jealous of his droopy vision, unable to believe if there's such an ailment.

Ramirez grunts and comes. Then he arches his back, shifts his weight next to me, his skin moist with sweat and pleasure. It's strange, this movement of visions: the changing color of his hair with light and the width of his wrists, his fumbling fingers on his iPhone. E-mails, texts in black and white, the rings of Saturn as his screen saver. He talks about the sixty-seven moons of Jupiter, the ones he has seen: Europa, Callisto, and Io from the observatory in his home. He describes their shape and diameter, the cratered ice and sulfur, the colors that have no names, the spectrums we cannot see. I recall the colors of my last meal, salmon pink and arugula green on a crisp white plate. Ramirez then turns and looks directly at me as if I am a distant object too. He is a muscled beauty. I wonder what size boxers he wears. I wonder if I should tell him about my blindness.

The room is half-dark and humid after he leaves. I turn my face to the window, not knowing when my blindness will return. A few fat drops of rain hit the glass and form veins of water running over each other. I walk towards the kitchen. The light drapes around me like gauze. There's salad, cartons of orange juice and milk kept side by side in the fridge. My hands inch towards a plastic bowl that seems to shrink and expand. I adjust my distance, even though I know it won't help. The blurred image is exhausting.

By the time I curl up on the couch, the rain is working hard on the roof. Maybe I should've asked Ramirez to stay. Clouds settle in my eyes. There is a color ahead of me I can't describe. The Discovery Channel is on. The narrator is talking about a species of sea slugs that discard their penis after sex but regrow it the next day. *Wow*, I say blindly, like a traveler who has found company.

When I wake up in the middle of the night, the blindness is gone. The TV is still on, and a dim light is seeping through the shades. Dr. Santoor mentioned my eyesight will recover once the blood supply to the optic nerve is restored, might take a few weeks or a few months. I think of my parents, who live in India, where it's sunny and bright right now, a large, blinking eye of land and sea that stretches between us with darkness and light trapped in it.

The cicadas are shrieking for company when I call Ramirez. In the distance the sky is clothed with golden light extending over the wet grass, the wooden fence, and the electric poles. I can tell he's staring out the window like I am, the phone cupped to his ear. *Callisto will be visible tonight; do you want to see it?* he asks. *Yep*, I say without any hesitation. A gibbous moon hangs at the horizon, dulled by the sun, and for some reason I imagine my mother growing fragile in my arms. The moons of Jupiter waxing and waning. The itch of color in my eyes vanishing after another instance of sex. As if none of it is real. Except that it is. Just like the blindness that'll follow. And the light that'll return, strangely renewed.

Isolation?

Cubes

During the day we work in the labs and at night we sleep on bunk beds in our cubes. Breakfast, lunch and supper are brought into conference rooms. Each of us is given a different specification to work on and we aren't allowed to discuss. There are cameras everywhere. We cannot leave this office until Project X is complete. Our families have received a shitload of money and all of us have signed a waiver.

Ken, my boss, works the hardest. I see him hunched over circuit boards in the lab, switching power sources, watching waveforms on the oscilloscope. He rarely eats. Sometimes I think he isn't real. Karen, on the other hand, is always in motion, setting up meetings, resolving issues with higher management. Her office has windows. I often stop by and look out. The world on the other side does not seem to care about Project X or us.

Gary sits next to me and gets up every hour for a smoke break. He talks to his wife while working on layout or studying schematics. I know it's her because he says, *I love you, bye*, before disconnecting. Then he kicks at the processor and mouths, *Piece of shit!* At night he sings lullabies to himself. I fall asleep listening to his gruff humming, wondering how much time has passed in this godforsaken place.

Every day I go through a new segment of code, line by line, and fix bugs. In between, I have revelations. The words come together and form sand on a beach or create a mountain. I imagine swimming far away from them. Or rock-climbing until I slip and fall—and the words revert to lines of code, a language whose purpose eludes me.

After 10:00 pm, Karen comes to collect data from our desktops. I can recognize her silhouette. Her high heels click and she sighs as she enters information in her handheld while I pretend to be asleep. She has administrative privileges. One day, I want to be in her position, able to control some number of things, able to say what I like.

I talk to my family via Skype or WhatsApp. My parents are always smiling, drinking wine, wearing expensive clothes. Sometimes when they don't answer, I feel I don't exist anymore. In the bathroom mirror, I'm often startled to notice myself, a woman who has a pointed nose, high cheekbones and light bouncing off her curves. Those nights I touch myself. The air above me illuminates like sections of code I've been working on. It seems beautiful and wrong all at once. A few times, I feel as if Gary is watching. I'm worried, some day he might come over and do things that I won't be able to resist. He might say, *I love you.* I wouldn't know what to say back—even though it's against what we signed, and our cubes are fingerprint-protected.

Our days look the same, feel the same. I think I'm getting used to all the quiet here, the fluorescent lights, the bright monitors displaying color-coded AC/DC signals. Maybe this is what death will be like—endless toil. The circuit board inside you rattling loose, a million lines of software in every cell pushing boundaries you've set for yourself, like this cube, this office, this body, this world. Another Project X in the works.

Except with more grace, innovation.

Mumtaz In Burhanpur

The girl, a tour guide in Burhanpur, India, has never seen the Taj Mahal, doesn't intend to. She's twenty, banana and history in her teeth. "Burhanpur," she explains, "is the city where Mumtaz Mahal died during her fourteenth childbirth."

*

She kisses a boy from a group of tourists, the sun beating on their backs. Along the rutted dirt road, she hums a ghazal, smokes a joint with the boy. Later, she points her stoned finger to the initial grave of Mumtaz before it was moved to Agra.

*

The girl has a tattoo of a rose-water fountain behind her neck. The boy licks her inked skin, his tongue drawing a map of river Tapti on whose banks the mausoleum was supposed to be. She feels as if her heart has been hoisted like a flag by the riverside, fluttering in the uncertain summer air. A kaleidoscope of rhythms.

*

Sometimes the girl dreams of Mumtaz. The empress tells her, "Death makes you larger than who you are." The girl thinks she embodies the spirit of Mumtaz—an embarrassment since she doesn't know Arabic or Persian languages like the illustrious queen did.

*

The girl's room is papered with sketches: Mumtaz practicing her hunting skills in her favorite deer park, Mumtaz relaxing in the Zenana hammam, Mumtaz wailing while delivering her last daughter, Shah Jahan coming to her grave, sobbing while reciting the fatiha.

*

A week later, the boy starts calling her Mumtaz—the name falling on her ears like a wish, as if her real name was never enough.

They're lying on her bed when she queries if Shah Jahan had other lovers, if he was capable of such devotion despite all temptations. The boy stares at the ceiling. Then he pulls up a blanket and says, "There's only one way to know."

*

The boy declares he'll mourn for a year, just like Shah Jahan did. He'll never marry. The girl feels a fresh fear, a giddy feeling of unknowing when the boy hands her a gun—the cold barrel drawing her in like a black hole. She realizes for the first time she's afraid of being buried. The voice of Mumtaz Mahal hovers over her, loud enough for clarity— "now I'll never leave

Burhanpur." Nine hundred kilometers away, the Taj Mahal glows under a full moon.

We're Waiting to Hear Our Names

We're kissing in the back seat of his '86 Chevy. Two country songs down and we're still locked in each other's mouths like lightning and thunder.

We're leaning against our Chevy, its front hood up. Cars, freight trucks slam by, weakening whatever honeymoon excitement still holds our dust-dimmed minds in caucus. We're waiting for the AAA, roving the radio dial: *Keep the Baby* hotline, punk rock, and weight loss pitches. We're getting into an argument. We're looking at the horizon where the light scatters and fills the stars.

We're rocking our twins, a boy and a girl. We're dreaming with them, without them, swimming in a space where we're popular names scuba diving in Hawaii and writing our love song in Bali.

We're spending Christmas with my in-laws; we're buying a thirty-year-old two-bedroom home that needs a clean carpet and a washer. The choices offered and the choices made, the No Man's

Land between them where we stand. We're standing next to the lawn mower, arguing whose turn it is. We're our hurried sex and laundry inside out. We're Children's Motrin in several flavors; we're bunk beds withering into nights too short.

We're still dreaming, riding bicycles, hair blown by the wind, cheeks red with sunlight.

We're walking to school, driving our kids to games. We're trying a new hair color, getting attracted to other men and women.

We're baking cookies and cleaning the grill. We're welcoming our kids and their fiancés. After they leave, we're sitting on the couch together in silence. We're going up and down the stairs. There're only crumpled sheets and time waiting in every room.

We're yoga in the morning, lumpy fried potatoes and meat with greasy throats in the afternoon, TV's blank face in the night. We're fixing the roof, changing the wallpaper. We're growing stingy with love. We're thinking of getting a divorce.

We're waiting for the doctor to tell us how bad it is. We're lying in the bed nestled with a drip. We're asleep on the rocking chair next to the bed, an unread novel latched to our chests. We're getting used to the sound of the heart monitor, the sight of life flickering against time, the growing knots in our stomachs. Sometimes, we're trying to laugh, laugh hard. We're lighting candles, thanking God for all we have, thinking we never really had a chance.

We're waiting for our turn to speak at the funeral, to talk about those moments of intermittent joy. Signing the paperwork, we're lonely below the dotted line. We're moving into assisted living, our kids, and grandkids waving at us, belted and secured in their SUVs, eager to leave. Wheel-chaired outside we're talking to ourselves, watching the onyx sky lit with smoking streetlamps.

We're lying in our graves separated by five years. The dirt is full of answers. Sometimes, we're whispering each other's name, and the dry flowers above us stir. And we're dreaming and waiting. We're waiting to hear our names.

resurrection

New Old

Before your mother's death, your father sat anywhere in the living room. Afterward, he'd place himself where he could see the urn holding her ashes. One day, he scoops out a tablespoon of ash and mixes it with his tea. Then he sits outside, up to his face in the pink evening as the light falls away.

A week later, when your father starts wearing your mother's saris and polishes his toenails pink, you tell yourself his transition is no longer a temporary one. He's still grieving, a relative says. Let him be.

One day, in the bedroom, you notice him blinking his kohl-lined eyes, the sparkle of your mother's mangalsutra on his neck bobbing a flash on the walls.

What're you doing? you bawl.

He shrugs, applies a coral lipstick on his dark, thin lips and smacks them together. His hands look worn and you wonder if they can cook fluffy puris and bouncy gulab jamuns, feel warm against your cheek, any time of the day.

Late that afternoon, he's changing into her silk blouse and you realize you've been wearing the same clothes every day. You look at his face—it's covered in foundation. The sari tied around his paunch and over his skinny legs has thin, pinned pleats. The little curly hairs on his arms and big toes are gone.

He asks you to watch your mother's favorite cooking show with him. Chickpea curry and bhaturas. He says he'll try the recipe. On the show, the fermented bread puffs in the fuming oil. A new old kind of transformation.

When do we distribute her ashes in the Ganges? you ask, your mind going straight to the urn.

He clears his throat. Her golden bangles on his arm jingle. We don't need to, he says, creating anxiety as you imagine your mother swimming in his veins, blooming, rising behind the whites of his eyes, wanting to come out, wanting to stay in.

Nine Openings

After the spacecraft crash lands in our backyard, we pull out an alien, its freckled, grey skin smelling like wet shoes, its oval, lidless eyes darting a glance on our foreheads. I inspect the capsule, the size of our compact car, shut dead. In your arms, the alien curls, a large bean. It draws out a tentacle, smooth and restless. The tentacle has an opening that blinks like an eye, raises like a fist, and we can't help but wonder at possibilities.

After the alien steps inside our house, something stirs behind its gaze—subterranean and sunken. Clocks stop and lights flicker. It lies down on the bed, between us, and the walls close in, making us touch. It pushes its tentacle into one of our nine openings and we're live wires, humming, twitching—a wave of ecstasy up our spine. Its slime smeared inside out, our skin neon pink—an electric fabric.

After the alien penetrates us, we lose our appetite. The fridge is stacked with ham, bread, and juice, but we don't open it. Outside, nothing changes, the same orange sludge smeared across the sky, bright and blistering. The alien nibbles on our shadows. Each appendage it licks disappears from our bodies, the wound sealed by its tentacle. After a week, it has my left ear, your toes—stiff organs pasted on its periphery. We stop fucking each other, we rarely speak, miss work. We're glued to relentless inserting, giving, forgetting.

After our limbs are gone, it's impossible to carry the alien. We push ourselves, inch towards it, crave for the proximity and shudder in fear, thinking what might happen when we have nothing left to offer. Its magic fin is our drug and we're crack whores.

After countless hours, the alien has more freckles than before, little craters of fire. Our body parts on its surface have decayed, fallen off all over the house. No matter how scorching, we fight for its tentacle and insert it into whatever is left of us. The heat drills into our cells, welding them into new structures—creating space, space between spaces, large pits of unknown.

After the alien dies, we try to consume its tentacle but it's a slab of rubbery meat, nothing left to give. The clocks are ticking again. A warm hunger rises in our gut and mists our eyes. Licking our lips with anticipation, we slump next to the closed refrigerator—our torsos seeping with mucus and blood under a harsh glow of light. Pleading and guilty, startled by our own voices, we feed on each other's shadows—dark spots on the floor, shrinking. Skin against skin. Ruptured white from inside, our flesh clings to the bones guarding the prune-shrunk hearts, wanting the burn in our chests to go away, the lights in our eyes more distant than the stars.

Poison Damsels in Rajaji's Harem, 1673

Sheila smiles, she's new in the harem. Her skin is smooth as ivory, her voice sweet as a koel, her waist curves softly. I want to take her away from Rajaji—the owner of this harem, the one with smallpox lesions on his face, the one who flicks his tongue like a snake. The king of this city. I massage Sheila's wet scalp with jasmine oil and braid her hair, a custom for new courtesans. She picks up the hookah, brings it close to her face, inhales the opium. I tell her she needs it, especially with all the tattoos she wants.

opium

I had a name once. Everyone in the palace started calling me Anokhi, the exotic one, as I was the first poison damsel. I was raised on a carefully crafted diet of poison and antidote from a very young age. The six other girls didn't live. Since then my body is a chilly oven of lust and death, never love.

poison antidote

Sheila stares at the ceiling while I get to work. Slow carvings on her luminous skin, a lotus garden on her back, a lair of snakes on her wrist, and a shadow of a goddess below her navel.

Anokhi - narrator

The tip of the needle dipped in poison and dye, my unwavering eye and her skin like Thar Desert under a summer sun.

I pour a glass of water and mix a light sedative. She gulps it. I watch her fall asleep, her arms overhead, and her chest rising and falling like waves in a sea. Later in the evening, listening to old ghazals and watching Sheila dance, I laugh with a surprising lightness. She smiles and I realize I've been thirsty for her clear-eyed, joyful way of looking at me. She's the place I've been searching for to call home.

"Anokhi Di," Sheila hollers.

I tell her to rest; the previous night was her first time, with a landlord, a bald man with a paunch, a rival of Rajaji. I place my hand over hers, cup her half-hearted compliance and try to remember what it was like before my body was blitzed with poison—free to love and surrender. But nothing comes to mind.

Sheila wakes up screaming. "I killed the landlord," she sobs, "with a kiss, Di." I take her in my arms, her narrow wrists tucked between our bellies. Ten minutes. It's the longest time I have been in such proximity to another human. "Shh," I whisper and rub her back, thinking of the two dozen men Rajaji invited to his palace over the years, rulers of small provinces on the outskirts of our kingdom. They passed out after my first kiss: a love bite on their inner lip, foam trickling from the sides of their pale blue mouths, merging our borders, expanding Rajaji's empire, robbing my conscience.

The next day, I take Sheila to a temple of Goddess Kali. I'm not religious, neither is Sheila. Perhaps I want to believe because I'm dying. Hakeem, the palace doctor, says long-term use of poison has hardened my veins, expanded my heart. I know Sheila's future is the same as mine, but prayer gives me hope.

She watches the dark-skinned deity, her arms fanned out, each holding an instrument of destruction. "She's like us," Sheila says and gazes out at the fields ahead.

"Not exactly," I say. "The Goddess protects the innocent."

When we walk back, the sun beats down on Sheila's pink face. In the distance a halo of dust rises in the fields surrounding the palace, quilting the green. "How do you feel now?" I ask, smoothing down her bangs.

"I feel fine," she says, removing my hand from her face and kissing it softly.

The world spins as I watch a serpentine sheen on her face and body. Sundazzled. She's nimbler than I ever was, more poisonous. And before I know it, I'm tracing my fingers on her blouse feeling her firm nipples. "Stop, Di," she growls. But I don't. We wrestle on the grass and finally, she sits with my head in her lap. She brings my face close to hers, breathing hard. I see her disbelieving eyes, desperate and worried. My nostrils flare to inhale her sweet scent. "Make me feel something," I plead, my neck cradled in her arms, my head a hive of buzzing desire before she breaks down and bites hard, somewhere close to my heart.

Whatever Remains

Mangoes are everywhere. On the tree, yellow and green, and on the ground, half-eaten, face down in brown red soil. They are on the roof, tumbling one after another, as the monkeys arrive in packs and shake the tree, their pink faces speckled with mango pulp and juice. We watch them from our bedroom window and wait for them to leave.

Papa was addicted to mangoes despite his high blood sugar levels. Every summer, he climbed the tree in our backyard and picked the ripe ones. Then he soaked them overnight, in water, before Ma decided if the mangoes were firm enough for fruit chaat, or soft and sweet for aamras—mango pulp, mixed with milk and saffron—or for mango lemonade. She sliced the leftovers for a spicy pickle. In long, warm afternoons, Papa sat in the courtyard holding a long stick to drive monkeys away. Ma sat next to him, singing his favorite folk songs, fanning a newspaper near his face. There never was a mango rotting on the ground when Papa was alive.

It was November when Papa's kidneys gave up. In his last days, he lay in his bed next to a window, his eyes closed, feeling the winter sun, hoping he'd survive one more summer. "I'll reincarnate as a mango tree to give it all back what I took in this life," he said before he died. Ma blamed mangoes for his death and forbade them in our house. Since then, once the monkeys leave the courtyard, we run outside and devour whatever remains.

Some monkeys are efficient. They suck the mangoes dry, lick the seed and toss them around, hitting other monkeys who drop the mangoes from their laps and run in circles. Some pick pants, petticoats and vests from our clothesline and wipe their sticky mouths.

One monkey catches us off guard. Unlike others, he's sitting on the ground. A few monkeys encircle him, their teeth busy, eyes at him. He's not eating. He doesn't even belong. We wonder how he has made it so far.

Humidity circulates inside our dirty, blue-colored home. We wipe the back of our necks, push our hair back and feel tempted to open the windows. Outside, the ruckus is on. Clouds are on the move, but, as per the newspaper, the monsoon is still a few weeks away. A dog whines in the distance. All we do is count the mangoes on the ground.

Later, Ma is awkwardly standing in the doorway that divides our house into two. All the monkeys have left except the odd one, holding a mango. She opens the window and the monkey glances at her, drops the mango, and runs away. She straightens, extends her gaze to the horizon and smiles at an assembly of dark clouds. We smile too, distracted from the fact that we need to go outside. For the first time in two years, like a girl wearing high heels for the first time, Ma takes a shaky step towards the courtyard, and unlocks the creaking door. A sweet-smelling silence extends between us. She almost trips on the slick seeds and ravaged mangoes while looking at the tree, humming a folk song, her black hair stuck to the side of her face. A fat drop of rain lands on her cheek. And as the world turns silver with rain, she slowly climbs the tree, towards the red, yellow and green ornaments hidden away from the reach of the monkeys, a spirit among them waiting to be released.

Spin

I fuck the girl in a restroom after work. In the corridors, a geologist on TV expresses concern about the slowing speed of Earth's rotation. We pull out plastic chairs, take sips from a Coke can. Walking back to our cars, I suggest my place.

At home I remove her foot. Carbon fiber. Precise. She suggests keeping the TV on while we make love.

"What might happen?" I ask.

"Tsunamis, hurricanes, all sorts of weather issues," she answers, her voice guarded, as if it's classified.

After she leaves, I marvel at how some things fit: the prosthetic with her body, her mouth and my tongue. My two fingers snug between her legs. Ins and outs.

How everything yields to a bigger force. Even Earth.

*

It's one of those pale, wrung-out Dallas mornings. We share a cigarette outside our office. She notices a bump on my wrist.

"Spider bite."

Her hand nudges my arm, her fingers like music on my skin.

Inside, on the TV screen, demonstrators are holding signs: Earth is tired of our weight. Let it rest.

That evening in her studio apartment, we fuck relentlessly.

*

An expert on the TV correlates slower rotation speeds to earthquakes, longer days and nights.

We feed on chicken wings, alcohol, and sex, wonder if our clocks are still true to their time.

I inspect the spider bite. It looks worse.

"You'll turn into Spiderman and save us." Her fingertips are curled around my ankle.

Whiskey blooms inside us.

*

Tonight, she's not exotic: It's cigarettes and family. A list of losses.

She says one day when she returned from school, her mother was gone; her dad was in his rocking chair reading *The New York Times* as if nothing had happened. So much went unacknowledged that year: her teen sister's pregnancy, the accident in which she lost her foot, mold on the bathroom walls.

"I always wanted to perform a basic two-foot spin on ice," she says. Then she increases the volume of the TV, punctuating the hum of disappointment.

I watch the smoke swirl around a completely still ceiling fan, realize my feet are cold.

*

She claims we'll drown in a hurricane; I bet it'll be an earthquake. We're afraid to say old age or illness: we'd rather be turned into stone. The sky is boring and blue. "It would be nice to travel somewhere," she says. I feel hungry for more of her, feel the vulnerability of our future. All at once.

*

Inside her apartment, I dim the lights. I move inside her like waves slapping against a marina. The skin on her face is redder, her eyes wormholes of scintillating gases. "Faster," she says and presses on the spider bite as if expecting a miracle. I pump hard, faster than a heartbeat, faster than a blink, our bodies like a top spinning in an unknown orbit, torching the air around us before slowing down, before giving up.

A Thousand Eyes

Rakesh runs his fingers on my midriff, warns about the humidity at this time of the year in Guwahati. Adjusting the pleats of my sari, I think about his mother. "As a newlywed, you should visit Kamakhya where Goddess Sati used to retire in secret to satisfy her amour with her husband, Lord Shiva," she said, her mouth drawn into a thin line, her chin drooping. I can tell she was beautiful once.

Goat scat shines on the hilly road. On the side, wildflowers entwine with weeds. We walk past the panels with sculptured goddesses, the *pallu* of my sari covering my nose, my anklets jingling, my thoughts absconding to the afternoon before the nuptials when I saw Rakesh's father with my neighbor, a widow of nearly ten years, in the back room, his hand caressing her back, his lips softly biting on her neck. Moans and whispers. Space filled with abandon. I felt hot behind my ears. I felt mysteriously hungry. For the rest of the day I couldn't decide if I felt outraged at Rakesh's father or lusted after Rakesh.

The sun burns behind the clouds, a subdued flame. A dull pain rises in the right side of my abdomen, as if something is released. I scan a dark indent at the horizon, wonder if it'll rain again, if the monsoon will leave us alone. After a while, the endless, relentless rain reeks, doesn't feel clean anymore.

The courtyard is streaked with animal blood. Offerings to the goddess include flower garlands, sweets and animal sacrifices. Sati is also famous as the bleeding goddess. She supposedly menstruates in the month of June and the Brahmaputra River near this temple turns red. In reality, the priests drop vermilion into the water to glorify Sati's fertility and fulfill the tradition.

Barefoot, the scat is pressed under our heels and stuck between our toes, some of it warm. A man, with a goat on a leash, turns a finger clockwise in his ear as he leads it downstairs to the sacrificing platform. My eyes are anchored to the animal's pleading eyes. A line forms and slithers towards the passage in the shape of a womb. At the entrance, the stone wall glistens as if engraved with a thousand eyes.

Rakesh holds my hand, looks at my feet. I study his sweat stained collar, his arms and his strong wrists. The air is weighed down by ringing bells. "I'll give you a bath," he whispers, his breath a flame under my earlobe. I wonder how long since his parents touched each other: if absence of fucking makes you stiff as a corpse, if lack of passion is mistaken for being closer to God. I wonder if this is the place to think of sex. If not here, then where?

Ahead of us, a pregnant woman tucks her hair behind her ears. A carving of another Goddess overlooks us. Garlands between her breasts, thick thighs, her skin grey, rubbed with time. A draft comes from inside the temple, warm as a tongue. The animal downstairs makes a sound, distinct like death.

I lift my saree that billows around my ankles. Chants drone on above us, the passage gets narrower and darker as if we are about to be crowned, as if we are about to be born.

When the line stops moving, I put my hand in Rakesh's side pocket, caress the fabric of his khakis. He places his hand over mine: his head slightly bent; his curly hair pointed at me. He resembles his father but clean-shaved, guilt-free. I want to tell him what I saw and felt: part rapture, part shame. In his brown eyes, I want to see my whole self and know if we'll ever have what Sati and Shiva had or if we'll drift away and I'll become compromising like his mother. If years will come out of us like colorful birds in the sky, or if they'll hang like roots of a banyan tree, limp. If one of us goes first, how will the other live?

Inside the cave, a sheet of stone slopes downwards from two sides, meets in a uterus-shaped depression. The Goddess is not a sculpture, but a stone kept moist from an underground perennial spring. The man, who came with the goat, makes his offering. A musty, sharp smell settles inside me. The pregnant lady bows, picks a flower lying next to the Goddess, and touches it on her forehead.

I close my eyes, fold my hands. And images crack open like an egg: Sati's mouth ringed with blood, the goat's head on a newborn, Rakesh opening and closing my legs, penetrating me in a hundred different positions. Bodies resting in dirt or washed off to the seas, corroded to salt. Bodies returned to stillness before they are done being dead, before they turn into pristine wombs and hearts, ready to be broken in again.

(handwritten margin notes: important village / fortune teller / killed by caring / daughter. She is / beheaded.)

The Fortune Teller

Mother touches their face and blinks like Morse code. No one understands her. I translate and do the readings for our tribe. Sometimes she picks up her stick and hits it on the ground. It is not just her voice and sight. She has lost much more than that.

Go home and stay indoors for a week, I say. If you must go out, always carry a weapon. I know every prediction is only for the time being. We all will die one day. Maybe because of too much sunlight or water. Or just love.

Mother was strong once. She could sniff the wind, look into my eyes and announce the danger. Now she only blinks and I am no longer sure what it means. Yet I keep translating. Maybe I hope to find something I do not expect. So, I make up stuff and tell them stories they have never heard before.

Cats know when an earthquake is coming, watch their tails.

The state of your heels reveals your sex life.

You will get better and live to see your grandson.

(handwritten margin note: fortune telling)

The dying embers of a campfire and their ashes in your backyard determine the health of your household.

And yes, time is stationary.

Often, I look at the sky. It looks like a crystal ball changing colors. I see shapes in the light, hear echoes in the wind. Ghosts trying to tell me something.

Mother has grown old. She cannot chew her food. I boil the meat, mash it with potatoes, and chew it for her too, so she can just swallow. Sometimes when I see her sitting or lying still, her mouth open, her eyes up in their sockets, I feel relieved that she has died. But the next moment, she exhales and starts blinking, fast. I feel guilty and happy, and in my large hand her palm feels like a bundle of twigs wrapped in muslin. I sing the song of our tribe and she stays still, her eyes closed, as if reciting a hymn.

The tribe respects us, especially after our rivals killed my father. The head of the tribe seeks counsel from Mother. While he is talking, Mother falls asleep. But he believes that she has been listening. That she will suggest the course of action the next day. He used to bring meat and vegetables for us. But lately, our predictions have been wrong, and he has stopped giving us food. We know that the tribe always needs a fortune teller, a reliable one. So, I sit next to Mother and hold her hand. The sky is blue with a wheeling cloud in the center. Mother opens her mouth, filling her appetite with air. We know what we need to do next.

She beats the stick on the ground and blinks. Steadily. You will always wake up knowing the answer. Don't lose it trying to find something that does not exist. The future that is, and the one we imagine, are as different as life versus a dream. And a good fortune teller always sees something that connects them.

In the evening, I give her a bath and dress her. Beneath the silk, there is a glimpse of her breathing. It will be cold soon. She moans as she lies down and I press my hands softly against her throat. She tries to resist my hands. But only a little. I close my eyes tight so that I don't see her face. The face I have loved all my life.

I sit still as I hear them coming. They are so close that I can smell their anger. The scent is older than anything I know. And I see the world fragile as an egg, the people in it trying to figure it all, making them believe that they can do something about their future. Arrows of predictions missing the eyes of fate.

I sense the blade on my neck, my pulse fluttering against the steel. And for the first time in my life, I feel certain as if I have always known this moment.

Snowstorm

The snowstorm sends us home early from work, so we fuck and sleep. When we wake, the power is out, and the room is a dark hole. We slip into sweatpants and over-sized shirts, pull up the shades to let in all that light reflected from white. The walls of the house seem thin, shivering. There are sounds we've seldom heard before—the wood cracking, as if giving up, a constant drip of water from the roof. We sit on the couch—tucked together under a blanket like children watching a scary movie. I say my mother lost me once on a crowded bus stop; you say you ran away from home, twice, and came back after a day. All along you'd been hiding in the attic. I say my parents stopped trimming my nails after my brother died. You say you were molested on a train, by a man your father's age. Then we go quiet; find our way through the dark to light the stove, make hot chocolate. I gulp the whole thing and want another immediately. Afterwards, I run my fingers over my crudely cut toenails. You reach an arm around my waist and suggest going back to bed. It feels like a good decision, because there's nothing else to do except watch the snow that falls relentlessly, burying everything we've worked so hard for.

Uncouple

When I was strolling outside that night, sleepless, the moon rolled down the hills and cracked open in the flat terrain between my home and the tree line. Rocks and baby moons embedded inside the sharp-edged slabs, cold and hard like glass. The night buzzed with loud insects and rustling leaves, a dog howled in the distance. I picked up a chunk—the size of a melon but twice as heavy as a bowling ball. Struggling to hold it, I stumbled back home and planted it in the yard, the air around smelling of wet wood. When I raised my head, up in the darkness, two stars blinked.

Later, I dreamt of the moonplant blooming, its sap rich and sticky as blood, its shimmering roots extending to the world's corners and edges, an underground Milky Way. I woke after my parents had left for work and flipped through the newspaper and TV channels, but neither mentioned the moon's disappearance. I rehearsed telling my best friend Shayla: her face weighed down by homework and absence of an ex-boyfriend, suddenly curious, her lips squeaking with questions.

When I walked into the yard, the sky was cracked with jet streams. The moonplant was glowing, pieces of quartz dangling like fruits. Leaning in, I saw sparkling orbits of flying debris, tiny fireworks underneath its membrane. Living, flashing, dying.

I touched the surface and it peeled like burnt skin. My soles lightened, a flutter rose in my stomach like when Shayla whispered a secret into my ear for the first time. I floated above the fence line, higher than the seams of the farmland, looking for her home. "Shayla," I called out, my voice sharp as broken glass, my arms stretched as if I were hugging the entire planet, my body an incandescent, shining crescent shooting sparks into the stars.

Only Buildings

Standing next to the microwave, I turn my head when my husband's phone buzzes. It's unlocked and he's in another room. Erotic texts and pictures of naked women. Redheads and brunettes, his favorites. When I confront him, he laughs, avoids the subject and takes me to bed. What is it? Am I not enough, I want to know, but his fingers flit inside me, purposefully. My head hurts, my thighs go slick. The room feels sour, the air shimmering like heat over a black cooktop. We go on, listening to the afternoon, the mindless twittering of birds, the squeezing, squishing sounds of our bodies as if raked from inside.

My husband is a construction engineer, travels for work during weekdays. He'd been married before. He said he loved his ex, an interior designer. They worked together. I've seen her photos on Facebook: spotless skin and earthy brown eyes. Dark, wavy curls. She looks like someone who smiles and gulps your despair.

My husband admits he has been with a lot of women while he was single, these women still reach out, send messages. Sex is like cotton candy, the more you have, the more you want, he says. He has done it at different times of the day and different places—airports, train stations, bus depots, office restrooms. Nothing surprises him much, he claims, and moves his calloused, large hands in the air as if raising a structure from rubble, a body.

The week after, my husband decides to work from home—an attempt to convince me he isn't fooling around. I walk past his home office, hear him clearing his throat while scheduling deadlines, managing material delays. Once, he excuses himself and takes a call on his cell—monosyllabic answers, muffled laughter, his sigh afterwards like wet concrete, yielding.

When my husband is traveling, I drive to an outlet mall near our home, buy lingerie and stop by Condom Sense on my way back. When the girl at the counter asks if I want to get the vibrator I'm holding, I put it back and pick the next one, higher power and wider, hot pink. There's so much I don't know. Belts, handcuffs. Support pillows for bones that angle in weird positions, bodies that open wide and swallow the light. That night, alone in my bed, I dream of my husband nuzzling between the legs of other women, their skin stubbornly white, their clits blistering pink. His tan body—an island between foaming seas. And I'm a surface of exposed metal beams with splinters everywhere.

The next time my husband is working from home, his office door is slightly open, his frame a dark rectangle filling in the space and shifting away. Other men and women are on speakerphone, their collective sound between him and the computer screen, the back of his nodding head, perfectly round, a dark blot in my dreams.

Quietly, I open the door and he turns around, his eyes shining like glass. He mutes the phone and pulls me towards him, the feel of his patterned t-shirt worn and soft against my face. He lifts my lingerie, presses his knuckles against my shivering hips, it's cooler in the office than the rest of the house, the seam of my thong snug deep. I like the scrape of his khakis against my legs, the shuffling of pages in the background, the incomplete floor-plans, the half-open window plastering morning on our faces.

He bends me over and rotates his hands over my round ass, bites my back. I laugh-gasp, my face hot with pressure and discomfort. He whispers in my ear to stay quiet, presses the mute button again and smiles thick, baring his near perfect teeth. The possibility he hasn't done this before makes me liquid. When I raise my gaze, I see the photo of his ex-wife in a small frame by his monitor, crimson lips, eyebrows perfectly arched. She's smiling, no grimacing. My husband's fingers reach deeper, and she starts to fade. The sun casts our jerking bodies against the walls like shadow puppets and I'm reminded of the pictures of women on his phone, the dark stain of their nipples, their mouths open, each letting out a ribbon of insulation around the words tumbling inside my throat. My husband talks about framing lumber and diagonal wind braces, his shoulders slightly heaving with our movements, his other hand slowly circling the mouse. In between he slow kisses my neck, a reward for my silence. Soon it fills my head, a floor rumbling, ready to give. When I finish, I moan and moan, wondering if it's my voice I hear—stretching thin and snapping like a building done wrong under a bulldozer, the ground emerging, spit crackle black.

Acid of Curiosity

growing up?

Inside my body, there is another body. _She_ has deep-set eyes, a nose like an inverted seven and a dark complexion. Her hands are stuck in my rib cage and her voice parades up and down my throat asking for Coke, chips, and internet. It's like being a building braced with dynamite. I bury the cans in the backyard and crush the chips and feed them to the squirrels, but _she_ finds out. Then _she_ screams and breaks down into small pieces like a mountain of LEGO bricks and I spend the entire day putting her back together. Glue and spit. Sometimes I can see her looking at me. Her radium eyes and glowing nails and hair, like a constant chemical reaction. Digits circulating in her body like blood. To calm her down, we go online and look for someone to talk to.

His name is Ryan. His picture looks like it was taken twenty years ago, but he says it is recent. His profile says, "Married but looking." Tonight, I'd rather sleep when he comes online (for the seventh time today), but _she_ wants to talk to him. Ryan likes to be up at night and talk to several girls simultaneously. We discuss our goals and aspirations. He says that he wants to be a firefighter. I hate to break this to him, but he doesn't look like one. When it's my turn, I sip my Coke while he chats with other girls and glances at me occasionally from his webcam, nods his head and says, "It's OK, take your time." Then he shakes his head and says, "My queen, your soul is divided."

My house once belonged to a musician. He is long gone but I hear him now and then. He sits in the attic and plays guitar. His voice is soft and swims in the air like perfume. He curses a lot and howls in his sleep. I imagine he is a person who has never apologized to anyone in his life. He walks barefoot with his guitar—its strings a part of his skeletal frame, and I can hear his feet pressed on the roof releasing a light rain of dust that settles in my hair. After he is done playing, he looks down and stares at me. Like the girl inside. Glowing eyes and teeth. And all I want to do is touch him and look into his eyes.

My parents think I am too fragile for a sixteen-year-old. They also think it will be good if I have a boyfriend. Like the girls in my class, who dream of a perfect SAT score and GPA, the right eye shadow, and a loyal jock as a boyfriend. None of them exists. At best it is a strange approximation. Predictable. For instance, I know, after a few minutes into my chat with Ryan, he will ask me to take my clothes off. He will go topless and play with his pimpled chest. Then he will remove his shorts and act like he is a lean, beautiful, and assured man. It's funny to watch him, because he isn't convincing in his act. He is over forty, but still a guest in his body. He is always performing. He looks exhausted.

On the other hand, I wear long dresses that drag behind me. My hair is limp and loose. I am a rag doll and I don't care much. I am comfortable even when I am tired. Of *her*. Of me. Of the tunes from the attic. But I don't wait for things to settle or change because they never do. Almost never. Instead life plays the guessing game with you. Sooner or later, you accept that misunderstood girl inside you and let *her* have *her* way. You find that odd note in the musician's voice and you start staring at the roof, intrigued. You catch that faint, hopeful smile on your parents' faces that says: *You are gonna make us proud, little girl.* And you feel accomplished as to how little they know you. How little you know of yourself. That this acid of curiosity keeps you going, making you believe—S*omeday I'm gonna figure this out.*

And at that moment, the girl and the musician become one. With you.

Subsong

There's a lady in the room. She is wearing a bikini, her nails painted black. Her ears are too close to her skull. She is looking out the window, gazing upon a pool boy, bare-chested and muscular. He looks up at her and smiles. It might be trouble, she thinks, and leans her head against the wooden frame. He wonders if she will smile and his eyes squint into the sun. His heart throbs when she smiles back.

There's a lady on an inflatable beach chair by the pool. Her skin is smooth, her eyes big and round watching the pool boy circling his tongue over her navel. The lady shifts her gaze at a cawing crow and laughs. She mimics a subsong: a low rattling courtship call among birds. The pool boy lifts his head and sees her open mouth, her syllables dispersed like pollen. The crow turns his head and flies away.

There is a lady in her bedroom, and she is sleeping. The curtains are drawn and faint moonlight shivers in. She is dreaming about the pool boy. He is between her legs and on her lips at the same time. She wishes the boy could go deeper into her skin, rake away whatever is left over from her last lover. And by the end of it she would feel like a clean pool, sunlight shimmering on her body.

There is a lady walking by the poolside, her breath heaving, and her skin paler than usual. She feels a kick in her belly and longs to give the baby a light squeeze. She wonders: if she does a subsong, will the baby hear? The pool boy is using a net affixed to a long pole to extract dirt and debris, light from the water dotting across his skin like Morse code. She waves at him, her stomach and hips pushing against the seams of her bikini. He smiles at her with a casual and distant politeness, his thoughts preoccupied with a girl he kissed last night. Before she dips her legs, she glances at the bottom of the pool. It seems shallower than it is.

There is a lady in the nursery. She is elated as she watches her baby napping, smiling occasionally at a dream. She has forgotten what the pool boy looks like. The days are shorter, filled with cidery smell and rich colors. Her body smells of breast milk and soiled diapers. Two crows on the maple tree branch closest to the window caw together. In the mirror she sees the stretched skin of her stomach and pulls it in for a moment, convinces herself she did it all for love. She laughs when the mirror blares that it isn't true. She decides to shave her legs and find her bikini. Poolside, she watches auburn leaves drift, gathering at the edge of the pool as if guarding the water.

Ghosht Korma

I dream about *Ghosht Korma*. Onion and garlic crescents shriveling in the fuming oil alongside turmeric and pepper smeared chops. The old Hindi music swirling like gossip in the street. I wake up and see a stranger glancing at my naked thighs. The heat is gathering and so are clients. Our mustard-colored room lined with nylon curtains is filled with naked bodies and obscenities. Rubina is up against the wall and Ganja, a local mobster and frequent visitor, is banging her hard. Her son, seven-months-old, is playing with the Housekeeper in the neighboring room. I'd like to talk to Rubina. But she isn't ready to leave.

*

Streets filled with hawkers and pimps. Bargains and thefts. Bees buzzing in every corner, laden with pollen. The giggling chicks with mismatched nails and second-hand stilettos. It isn't a cruel life, if you ask me. Although I haven't had any client in the past three hours. I listen to the splashing water—the flush and shower, rooms filled with fog. I occasionally catch the lucid faces of men burning with alcohol, rims of white powder on their nostrils as they pass by the room. I stand topless by the window. And I realize it's going to be another long day with no food. The Housekeeper always says, *Earn your meals*. My body gleams, my stomach hurts.

*

Yesterday, Julie mentioned strawberries. Hakim rubbed a few over her ass before fucking her. Solid stone without a beating heart. Julie is his favorite. He always rubs a pinch of cocaine on his teeth and hers, after he is done. He never laughs, snickers with his eyes. Reminds me of my mother. She rarely smiled. The creases under her eyes, her stubborn hair pulled by men she trusted. Her skin pale, a fading evening.

*

Diwali is approaching, the festival of lights. The triumph of Good over Evil. Last Diwali, we had a parade. I was dressed up like a monkey. Ganja made me walk on all fours all night long. The next evening, he sent a silk sari and two cones of ice creams. Since I spent the entire day breathing in *beedi* fumes and taking care of Julie who had been throwing up like crazy after Hakim forced her to eat rotten leftovers, the ice cream was a rare treat. It almost made me forget that Ganja picked me up by the park outside my home when I was twelve.

*

Outside, children play and laugh. Rubina is walking with her son in her arms. It is a gambling night at the House. I have to clean the kitchen, sweep all the rooms and wash bed sheets. It is tiresome but works like magic. Smooths my thoughts. It is time for the prayer call from the mosque. The Housekeeper says, *Prayers are useless,* and maybe they are. Rubina believes in God. I haven't decided yet. Sometimes I try to recall the life I once had. And I don't remember anything except my mother and her hands smeared with spices, preparing the best *Ghosht Korma* I ever had.

The Undecided Colors

We rode the bus all night long. Outside it was wet, the irritating summer drip. The bus felt safe and dry. Remy, my second cousin, drove it around the block and then went around the town in circles. Benches, lamp posts, schools and drug stores, occasional open fields nestled with puddles. We passed by the graveyard where his mother was buried. He slowed down but didn't stop. At the bus stop, some people screamed and ran after the bus. I rested my cheek against the window and laughed. It made me feel important and in control.

Remy was driving the bus for the first time. He let out a long sigh every time he turned and went over the curb. "Great timing, there's nobody on the road." His arm tattooed all the way down, his head angled as if listening to someone whispering a secret into his ear. He came back from Afghanistan not too long ago and smelled like a turned vegetable. He told me he'd smelled worse. I could tell he was better with cars.

Around midnight, the rain stopped, and the tar roads shone as if paved with diamonds. I thought about my mother; saw her face in the dark panes of empty buildings, her shadowed eyes fixated on me. I always thought she was depressed, the undecided colors in her eyes. And yet the only one who could see right through me.

Out the window, a cloud veiled a gibbous moon.

"How're you doing, babe?" Remy hollered and honked. "Fine," I hollered back. "I still see sand everywhere, the meds drive me nuts," he said. Then he raised his right hand and shook his fist at the night.

When I was twelve, my mother and I used to walk to the Hare Rama Hare Krishna temple downtown. Lunch was free on Sundays. I watched the bone-thin priests and eager devotees rushing through the corridors. There were the indigo-colored paintings of Krishna playing with his mother, Yashoda, whose face didn't look anything like my mother's face. But I hoped someday it might. The food tasted delicious after hours of walking. I felt sleepy on our way back and my breath smelled of potato curry and garam masala.

Caution, the yellow sign read as the bus rode up the hill. Even though I knew every bit of town, I wondered where Remy was going. Where he had been and why I was here with him at this hour. After a few years, I'd figure it out, I said to myself.

The trees on both sides of the road looked like ghosts waltzing in the pregnant air. I pulled out my cigarettes and walked towards Remy. The pale shrubs quivered as the bus drove past them and the headlights made small moons ahead. I could see Remy's face, flickering orange through the curling smoke, his left hand firm on the steering wheel and his steady, purposeless gaze. I wanted to know what he was running from.

Outside, a thin streak of light sliced the chest of darkness. For a moment, I didn't know who I was, or where I was. When it came back to me, I imagined my mother sitting at the kitchen table. She was waiting for me. Her face sagged around the edges with the weight of our failure in finding love. And I thought of Remy's tongue in my mouth, a whiff of his stinking sweat in a way I'd find both repulsive and attractive.

Hands

My father has large hands. When he moves them across the room, with his fingers apart, they fan my face. Often, I fill his palms with pistachios and cashews and eat them one by one, watching a movie on the tube. One night, in the dim light of his room, while my mother is away, I see his hands on the bare back of Lucy, our young, twenty-something neighbor. Twelve-years-old and startled by the intimacy they share, I storm past the front door and into the main street. I continue across uneven lawns, up and down the steps of the porches, climbing over curbs. Finally, I sit in the middle of the road, sobbing hard.

The next day, I wake up to the smell of omelet and baked bread. I walk into the kitchen; my father's hands are white with dough, his hair more gray than black, and his eyes, a warm shade of blue. He is the same. He isn't the same. It is as if he was reduced by last night's incident to someone I used to know in my bones. We pause, we look at each other, and before I close my eyes, I see him moving away in his muscular body, his hands shivering, his lips pursed tight as if pulled by a storm inside him.

For the next few days, propped up on pillows, my nose pressed between my knees, I stare outside the window. I watch the sun crawl up and sink down the cloud-ravaged skyline and wonder how small things have large consequences. The rest of the world goes on at a separate pace while I leave my room only to eat. I don't answer when I am spoken to, even though I feel like screaming. I listen to the sounds once the TV is turned off. The swivel of my father's oval-back chair, the car keys and coins he leaves on the kitchen counter. The rattle of his belt. The soft thud of his shoes hitting the floor. One night he enters my room, pulling the stool from under the lamp, and sits close to my bed, his hand next to my back. I can still smell the lunchtime beer on his breath. There is something else circulating in the air: a light sexual tension from me knowing his secret, my contempt for his desire, our combined shame. I want him to go. I want to turn around and hold his hand. Instead I stay still, my eyes shut, my breath steady, as if tightly wrapping my muscles over my bones.

Two weeks later, my father passes away in his sleep. His death certificate says Cardiac Arrest. I read it several times. My mother rings the bereavement services and goes for an oak-lined coffin because she thinks she knew my father best. I don't say a word. I stay up all night. I write. I give up cashews and pistachios. I spend my time looking at his things wishing they were gone too. My only sliver of comfort about his death was how everything is beyond damage and repair, how everything you value slips to vaguely important. Lucy stops by often, she brings food. I try to be as graceful as I can be, long before a time when I might be. Her eyes are red from crying and she looks startled, as if she woke up from a bad dream. I hadn't considered love.

Years later, I sit in a motel room feeling the hands of a man I long to be with, his wedding ring pressing cold into my freckled skin. Unsettled by the memories, I look up, stare at the mirror. And in the reflection, I see my father, raising his hands as if to stop me.

Infinite

He hasn't smelled my hair in a while.

He hasn't slammed doors. He just leaves quietly after a fight. And two meals later, both of us start talking normally as if disposing of the evidence of the last argument.

He hasn't commented on our updated relationship status on Facebook. But he was the first one to like it.

He hasn't shown me what he writes. Not all of it. Even when he does, I feel some of the words lift and circle over my head like air.

He hasn't used a separate blanket since last Thanksgiving when I had the miscarriage. He sleeps with his hands on my belly as if protecting everything that ever came from him.

He hasn't complained about the open toothpaste or my hair-infested combs lying in his drawers. He lets them mingle with his shaving brush. Like sharing the details our fingers cannot reach.

He hasn't fiddled with the remote while I am watching the tube. Perhaps it is a sign of giving in or giving up.

He hasn't locked his email since the last blackout, six months ago.

He hasn't presented me with a ring. But twenty-one months of sharing a toilet and closet space is as close as one can ever get to a marriage. They say twenty-one is the magic number to form or break a habit.

He hasn't refused when I suggested taking a sabbatical and going around the world. Even if it means staying sedated all the way because he is scared to fly.

He hasn't talked in his sleep. He hasn't given up smoking. Sometimes, I see him standing on the patio, blowing away rings of smoke, smiling to himself like a man who has finished his work, settled his debts. Like a man who is certain, yet soft as sky— infinite in its possibilities.

Measurable Hours

9:30 am – checking in at a hotel

The key unlocks a room with a twin-sized bed, orange wallpaper, and an over-sized dresser. Nick hands $5 to the bellboy and closes the door. I lay my purse on the dresser and tuck my loose hair behind my ears. He empties his pockets; iPhone, cigarettes and the room key end up on the side table. We are here next to each other. There is an inappropriate desire in his eyes as he runs his fingers through my blonde hair.

I know the floral pattern of his unbuttoned shirt: chrysanthemums on beige background. The colors go with his tan face and arms, the pattern with his wide, angular jawline. It makes me want to lick the skin between his shoulder blades.

11 am – lying in bed

There is a good smell in the air. An apple pie baking somewhere. Nick talks about his wife's latest plastic flower collection. I cringe, resist my temptation to get up while he stares at her pictures on his phone. I keep my leg over his thighs. He puts his phone away. His fingertips trace the curve of my flattened breasts and circle my left nipple. We curl into the blankets, whisper. Outside, the light thaws the shadows, misplaces a faded moon somewhere.

1 pm – room service

He looks pleased. I extend my hand and pull out a cigarette from the pack. Room service? In a veil of smoke, he orders two chicken sandwiches, a side of fries, two Cokes. This is the man I love, no, this is the man I love to fuck.

3 pm – strolling outside

We take the elevator down to the street. Crossing the busy roads, we hold hands, breathe in dust, merge with the fabric of the city. When he mentions his teenage daughters with a distant politeness, I think of my son's room full of scattered toys and open markers. A paper sign on his door and a family portrait on the side wall. I look like someone else.

We talk about my work, his recent investments, big data analysis, faux teak doors and an online store for handicrafts. Sunlight reflects from the multi-colored windowpanes of shops and parlors. In a world of infinite prisms, I feel like napping.

4:30 pm – the napping dream

I am naked in my bedroom with Nick. A torch of sunlight.

Our bodies become one. My son is playing in the yard and my husband is working in his office, sighing with a slight ache. I try to stop Nick, but he pins me down and enters from behind. We stay locked even after Nick stops moving. I try to uncurl because I know the door is open. But my neck cannot lift my head, my arms and legs remain stuck. I keep falling back to the bed releasing puffs of fatigue.

6:15 pm – awake in bed

Wrapped in a bed sheet like a burrito, I watch Nick, his knitted brows, his eyes staring at the laptop screen. He looks bigger, his legs stretched on the table, filling up the room.

I envy his productivity. Walking to the bathroom, the air feels heavy, pressed to my body. Underneath my breasts something beats harder. Between my shaved legs is a triangle of flesh that has become blind. Should we meet again is about to become an issue.

6:45 pm – dinner in the restaurant on the terrace

He makes a call, probably to his wife. I look around; we are the only ones here. Two waiters stand in the corner. I move my bangs away from my forehead, fake-focus on the laminated menu, wondering what my husband is doing right now, suddenly hungry for a wood-fired pizza.

8 pm – just before heading out

There is a roomy gap between him and our cabin suitcases. I settle there. He checks his phone, pushes it into the back pocket of his pants and hugs me. From the corner of my eye, I see the dark blades of the ceiling fan. Listening to his heart, I hear mine. I am thirty-nine, married with a son.

10:30 pm – on red-eye flight, dozing

Drifting away into another dream, I'm planting bulbs in my yard, my green gloves deep inside dirt, memories flowering on my back. I run inside. Past the screen door, my husband is waiting, the skin of his palms pulled to a slant as he extends his hand. I look him in the eye, match his smile, follow him into our story. Not speaking, just walking, trying hard not to look back.

Bikini Wax

Rosalina is Mexico pulled inside out. A striking woman, smooth as an olive, with a firm bun of brown hair. Desire on legs, whether she's pussyfooting between the rooms at the Salon or she's doing a Brazilian on a client under stark, fluorescent lights, patting the pussy, waking it up.

When I arrive after three months of growth tangled between my thighs, Rosa is busy with another client. I don't mind waiting. Other attendants pass by. I hold their faces for a moment. Nice girls. Girls waiting for someone. A man or a woman, doesn't matter. Not Rosa. She's here even when she isn't.

When the door opens, a twenty-something girl walks out. Rumpled hair and flushed cheeks. I walk in and Rosa hugs me, the smell of her lavender shampoo tickling my straight bearings. She replaces the sheet, sprays the room with Lysol, and adjusts the TV. A busty Latino is singing.

"Long time." She sticks a towel between her breasts and helps me undress. A layer of wax glistens over my pubic bone like molten gold. I tell her my husband is traveling again, the last trip to India seemed so long and my swimming lessons are going well, as if I have promised to disclose all the details of my life. She talks about her ex-boyfriend whose last name was Ali. He was a carpet weaver from Iran who liked to have burritos and pancakes for breakfast. They had sex every single day when they were together. Sometimes even three times a day. One morning, the immigration authorities took him away. He never came back. She presses the strip and pulls hard.

"Shit." I bite my tongue.

"He coming soon?"

"Who?"

"Your husband? You have someone else?" She laughs and the luster in her eyes deepens as she wipes the exposed skin and applies moisturizer, slowly circling from my navel to my clit. I see her arched eyebrows, sweat trickling down her neck, her frame oscillating between hurt and pleasure, and I feel words rolling on my tongue and falling back, sticking in my throat.

"Take your time." Her voice cracks. She pats down my pussy, her fingers groping the flesh for reassurance. I try not to think of my vacant home, my absent husband, the swimming lessons I don't go to, and the vacation that never happened. I'm wet, maybe even smelling. The room is like a void, nothing but a knot of excitement in motion. This is the real thing. I repeat it quietly. I'll never come here again. I'll come here again and again and again.

The girl on the TV is still singing.

Feeding Time

Almost spring, and a sparrow hits the fan and falls into the mutton curry while we're having lunch. Papa says it's something to do with feeding her chicks, the bird's always in a hurry. I pick up and carry the stunned little creature to the bed where Papa and Ma don't sleep together anymore.

Year after year these sparrows have been making nests in that corner of the living room—one morning a broken egg on the floor, yolk clinging to the fractured shell. The same week Ma woke up in a pool of blood and cried for weeks because it was a boy.

Every few days, Ma cleans the bird shit stuck on the floor and the wall. Back in the nest, the mother's at attention, a rush of wings as if responding to Ma's curses. Some days the sparrow sits on the fence, flies around, swoops this way and that, shows off.

Now the bird lies on her side, breathing hard, until she puffs her gravy stained chest and stands up. Before I help Ma to dispose of the mutton curry—the only food we had because we're down to single meals a day since Papa got fired last month, I check on her again—and sure enough she's back in the nest, peeping at our empty dining table.

What Might Come After You

It is early afternoon when I decide to rearrange your closet. The sun is kilted with clouds, spouting heat on the far end of the horizon. I glance at the bathroom mirror and see the dust assembling into a portrait of our relationship.

I fold your slacks, pair the slippers, and pick up newspaper cuttings. I imagine you standing here not too long ago with frowned eyebrows over round, gold-rimmed glasses settled on your Afghani nose and striped pajamas below your dense belly, holding a bunch of pages and a pair of scissors. For me, you were not made of bones and blood, but alive with head-to-toe contradictions and rare, loving glances in your curious eyes. Your long torso and broad shoulders carried the weight of our dead and only son and later my pounding fists when you could not bear to see me beating my chest anymore. Your feet occasionally scratched and bled my skin, waking me up when I sobbed in my sleep. You soothed me with plush fingers that wove intricate designs on high quality wool and silk. Your rugs were as conceited as your glare after a hot day had passed with good food and satisfying sex.

Often, you looked like my father, bulging with the confidence of knowing everything. You had strong hunger and it reflected every time you got up from the dinner table blurry eyed and confused, even after consuming a full meal.

I sift through the shirts that are older, and dear to you. One of them has a blood stain from the day when you accidentally cut yourself. It was the same day you found out you had diabetes. You cried like a baby.

You said, "I was fighting the unfairness of life with sugar and Allah took my candy."

I watched you the entire day; I followed you in your studio as you pulled and pushed silk between spaces where stubborn air accumulated. As far as I know, it was the only day when you did not pray.

Once, I had a dream in which your desire swelled like a huge tongue devouring a mountain of sweets in one swipe. When I woke up, you were unusually calm, as if the dream was real and your willingness to indulge was a way to convey your grief.

Diabetes did get the best of your body. You filled the studio with unfinished designs, aimless threads. You stayed in bed most of the time, pretending to be asleep. When the midday glare settled into soft pink evening, you asked for minted iced tea and speculated on what you might like for dinner. After a month, on a quiet Ramadan evening, you passed away, your eyes half-open, staring at the picture of our son with a faint hope. I stood next to you watching your frame as if I didn't know who you were.

As a couple, we led each other into our hearts and stayed there for a while. And in some frivolous moments, I realized my love for you. The rest of the time, I tried to understand my devotion, but took it as a byproduct of being married to someone for a long time. However, you always loved me with a constant fervor, sarcasm, and anger. During my frequent outbursts when I cursed our marriage, you always corrected me: "Fight with *me*, Begum, not our relationship."

I open the trash bags and stuff your belongings inside; catching sight of the chenille duvet we bought in Cairo. The one for which you bargained for hours. When I called it a labor of someone's love, you exclaimed, "Begum, it's just a duvet!"

"It is more," I fumed, trying hard to dismiss you. "But what would a rug weaver know of love?"

You wrinkled your nose. "How else would a weaver push those threads into places where it hurts the most? But in the end, it's just a rug, sold for the right price."

I push the duvet into the trash bag. And like a torn page from a history book, I try to anticipate what might come after you. It's like watching dappled sunlight play across a dense forest floor, not knowing which leaf will blaze and which will stay in shade, hoping to be discovered.

A Closed Circuit

My husband says I am out of love. He claims there is an empty space two fingers down my ribcage where love used to be. So, he goes out with other women. When he returns, he cleans the house, puts on music, showers for a long time. His skin glows, his teeth shine. Sometimes my husband cries and talks in his sleep. I interlace my fingers with his and whisper, *I understand*. But he pulls away as if he can't stand the vacuum that oozes out of me. Lying next to him I smell a woman I used to know but can't recall her name. Was it Claire, Judy, Raina? Doesn't matter, it makes me wild, it turns me on: this dream, a culmination of all the women he has loved. It fills the void, makes me giggle. My husband wakes up, presses his hand under my bust, feels the flutter and confesses he does it all for us, to feel this moment together.

Sometimes the dream rises like smoke from my husband's cigarette, forms a funnel, a cone of faces revolving around him. Blondes, redheads and brunettes. Lost and beautiful. When my husband emerges, he looks brand new, like a man ready to seduce again. He dyes his hair, wears contact lenses, and finds a different girl. Buys her expensive clothes and jewelry, slow dances with her until she cracks open like an egg and spills her cravings in a cheap motel in the middle of nowhere. He brings her home. Together they watch movies, eat popcorn and fall asleep on the couch. I slip away from the house into the streets and parks, washed in loneliness, sitting in my car, as the dusks flow into nights. My husband swears he never makes love to other women because he wants to stay loyal to me. *Commitment is what we live for*, he says. Eventually, the girl leaves him. Her scent, her longing to find true love, her wish to be remembered, all become a part of the dream.

The dream gets stronger, its grip tighter around our souls. A closed circuit.

My husband asserts he wants me to get better, to become a woman whose body is a large, beautiful bird: soft and accessible, whose heart explodes with love and understanding. The hope in his eyes makes me dizzy. I carve out cardboard wings, attach them to my loose kaftan and flap in front of the mirror. I try to feel a movement in between my breath, a rush of color on my cheeks. Nothing. Usual rise and fall of my chest. *Thump thump* of my heart. The woman in the mirror raises an eyebrow at me. In the background, my husband winces.

Five weeks in a row, my husband gets red roses for the girl he is seeing. I soak in the warmth of their rich color that rises like a giant bubble and settles in the empty space inside me. *I'm making progress*, I exclaim but he doesn't believe me. *The dream is the cure*, he says, running his fingers over a rosebud, tight and tender like a rolled tongue.

My husband takes a break between dating girls. Those nights are the hardest. I ask him about signs of love and his silence sweeps through me. As days go by, I feel less sure about who I am. He promises things will recover. One day, he'll hold my hand for hours, paint my fingernails, massage my scalp, tongue-kiss between my legs, raise kids. The way he says this makes me believe it. Or want to.

Intermittently I worry if we'll run out of girls, if my husband will no longer have the passion to fill my bareness. If I'll never carry in my womb what I want to know about love and pass it on. But he is always ready as if there is nothing else for him to do. As if finding another girl is as involuntary as his breathing. As if he needs the dream more than I do. As if I'm not the one out of love, I never was.

Between Not Much and Nothing

After my mother died, my father removed the batteries
from every clock in our house, adjusted their hands to the time
when my mother was born, when she married my father, when she
gave birth to me, when she died.

My father claimed he dreamt of my mother every night:
sometimes by the lake, her lilac sari lifted up to her knees, her feet
burrowed in warm sand. Or at a party, walking up to him in her
flowing, off-shoulder dress, bright lipstick and heavy European
perfume he'd never approve of, asking for a slow dance. Or lying
in a hammock outside our home, an over-sized hat over her
face, _Anna Karenina_ resting on her chest.

I shrugged a lot, I let him be. Kissed him on his forehead,
said I was sorry, and switched off the lights of his room. And my
father's eyes were half-open, staring at the moon, a little patch of
white in a dark space.

My father slept more. When he woke up, he cried. I
waited for him to stay awake for at least a few hours a day, even

though I knew he was less lonely in his dreams. But he stayed in bed, snoring, sobbing or talking to my mother—between not much and nothing.

"Mom never went to parties or had a hammock," I told him one of the few times he was up and lucid.

"I know," he said, "but she always wanted to."

Now his first death anniversary dawns grey in the still house. I dig through the closets, bring out the sleeping clocks, push the batteries in. Watch their crawling hands. The creaking door opens to the bedroom where I can see my father rising from his bed where he died sleeping. I imagine my mother snug in her grave. The sound *tick tock* fills the room. Something happening, something passing.

Clueless

[handwritten annotations: "transplant heart left in restroom" and "women scared"]

There was a line outside the women's restroom. Inside, someone had left a human heart in a transplant container. Women who'd seen it described its shape like a fist: brown with blue stinking edges, pipes in and out, like old-fashioned plumbing. The heart had spoken to them about their past, they'd seen it twitch, flip a beat.

A woman sobbed inside and a chill spread through the line. Outside, in the parking lot, the August light whited out all the vehicles. When she emerged from the bathroom, she claimed the heart was watching her while her hands shook, her ears rang. She felt older and tired in its presence as if her own heart wanted to stop and stay still.

I'm scared, exclaimed a young girl, her forehead beaded with sweat. A blonde who visited the heart twice, twitched up, leaned towards the girl. *There's nothing to worry about*, she said. *What if the heart knows my thoughts,* the girl asked. *It's possible,* the blonde replied.

[handwritten annotation: "fear superstition"]

Two women in flannel shirts decided to go in together. The stark brightness of the bathroom flashed for a moment. The power flickered. *Must be the heart,* a black woman whispered. Another female suggested making an offering to the heart. *It's that time of the year when the spirits descend,* she said with a nod of familiarity while collecting money to buy Snickers and bottled water. A police car and an ambulance stopped at the entrance of the building.

The officer urged everyone to go back to work. The white-gloved attendant grabbed the transplant container and rushed back to the ambulance.

The blonde and the sobbing lady tightened their lips, looking beyond the ambulance merging with the traffic as if committing something to memory. They thought they'd found the roundness love is supposed to bring, they'd put it to greater use. They'd understood how a heart, snug in its own body, found solace in its constant rise and fall, but now, after a face to face with the heart in the transplant container, they realized they'd no idea at all.

Egress

It is early evening in the sky and in my palms. The sand sticks to my toes and rubs memories into my skin. The water in the lake shivers to the beat of heat and wind.

I close my eyes and think of you. Five ten, thick beard, eyes green like the Arabian Sea; the way you always rose from next to me and took up all the space in our bedroom. The way I dreamt of marrying you because I wanted to be with a man who'd trek for miles or travel for days like it was nothing, or who'd come to India and understand how I'd feel after visiting a child, the one I sponsor, in the slums of Kolkata. Who'd open his arms as if he was about to embrace an ocean. The one I'd never love as a friend or kiss on the cheek, but someone who'd know what my body would ask of him whenever I'd blush and look away. But you remained a brilliant flash under the water and I raised above the current, like a rock, familiar and nearly forgotten, each crevice on my skin an extension of your touch.

A few kids have spread out their toys. Their colorful swimsuits stick to their rounded bottoms and shower sand as they get up and run towards their mothers wearing hats and shades, sitting still in the sun, wondering how they arrived here.

The last time you called, six months ago, was from another coast, far from mine. You said you spent the whole day watching the waves with a girl much younger than you. And I tightened like a muscle even though we'd broken up a year ago. I dug a deep hole in the sand and buried the notion of how together we'd always fit. How we'd always be a force: similar education and world views, morals, never competing. Yet today, I raveled like a river—unearthing and rinsing every dream, every thought with hope and fear, gazing at those kids in between, wondering how I got here.

Inside the cabin, I wash my feet and watch the sand go down the drain. Your message displays on my phone. Maybe you are digging up memories too. Maybe you think you can reel me back in—that part of you that keeps reaching out to me, apologetic and hesitant: *how are you, how is work,* before you proceed to talk about yourself. I toss the phone on the bed and open a window. A draft comes in, warm as a tongue. From far away, I hear a diesel engine. The kids are gone—their toys half buried in sand like broken hearts.

Outside, air shimmers between the water and the purple horizon. I wonder where I'd go next. Another room by a sea with the same colored sheets that smell of damp towns, a jug of light by a single bed, closets with two hangers, big enough to hide. No carpet. A muted television. Wet between my fingers, sand between my toes, hair frizzed up in humidity.

I light a cigarette and hum our favorite song. My body shivers before all of you come out as long white smoke, evaporating, lifting a veil above a blackness that slowly seeps and spreads inside me.

Milk Chocolate Messenger Man

I adjust my spaghetti straps and glance at the minibar inside room 206. Colored, skinny bottles like manicured fingers. From the window, I glance at the afternoon sun dulled by gory clouds with rain on their backs, a lemon-grey canvas over columns of speeding cars.

David slides his hands across my waist interlacing his fingers with his wedding ring on top. "You've led the stormy weather here," he smirks. His old hat is an odd touch to his blue shirt and black jeans. But the grin is center stage. This is the first time I am with him and he looks like a man with lively blue eyes, who works from eight to five—someone who can afford a bit of nonsense. We are in a hotel right across the highway, next to the airport. Thunderstorms weren't in the forecast, but I can smell them heading our way.

Dim daylight. Faded darkness. I remember Dolly, my friend, casually mentioning how she fucked a middle-aged banker, Tom, for a couple of twenties. Tom even cuddled her afterwards.

A few nights he even took her out and opened the door for her. After half-a-dozen heartbreaks and the itch to have bigger things which my waitressing job cannot scratch, I thought it might be nice to have what Dolly had. However, she made me promise not to make a habit out of sleeping with strange men. "Once that indifferent girl settles beneath your skin, you are unstoppable," she said.

"How are you," David asks with a prepped tone and takes his hat off. I can feel the glare of his stare. It says: *I am hungry and bored. I ache and yearn to be noticed.* He grins and I see a dimple in his left cheek, his ears turning red. It seems as if he is about to say something. Outside, the clouds are gathering to spill rain. The lines of buildings and bridges are blurred. Inside, the light is bright and reflecting off our bodies, creating an awkward fizz.

"What's this?" I pick up a small box placed near the TV, next to the roll of *USA Today*. The label on the box says, *Milk Chocolate Messenger Man*.

"Let's see." He lifts his eyebrows, extending his forehead to the receding hairline as if he is checking a balance sheet. His ears, erect, move away from his face, curling a little to pick up the crackling sound of cellophane.

"It's milk chocolate with almonds, baby." He holds it out. His voice has a light, gravelly undertone. Seedy and affectionate at once.

I pop a brown, leathery square into my mouth and sit on the edge of the bed sweeping the inside of my cheek with my tongue. He draws the tan-colored curtains and loosens the belt under his paunch. His naked profile—an interesting combination of large shoulders and small hips—moves towards me. His skin is coarse, his chin strong and his lips pursed tight. I think of his wife, possibly average looking, wearing sweatpants and loose T-shirt, standing in a grocery aisle picking up pasta. Or at home reading a magazine with fuzzy instructions on interior decoration. He pulls up the comforter, releasing a fine layer of dust between us. An airplane drones above our heads sucking a hole of air and I imagine all the passengers and the crew looking at us. There is a familiar face among them. The face of my mother.

He cups my breasts, pulling down my tank top, and his wide thumbs press my dark, upright nipples. Then he kisses me as he unbuttons my shorts. I notice the tense muscles in his shoulders extending to his neck. There is no sound except that of the air conditioner wafting along our bodies. He moves fast inside me, supporting my legs over his shoulders, groaning with quick satisfaction.

"You're sexy, Nora," he manages to say in between his panting and hurried movements. And I realize that he has not fucked many women. When he comes, he lets out a small sigh and looks down as if ashamed of himself. Then he withdraws slowly and grins. I wonder if he will say something now.

He adjusts the pillows in an L-shape and lies down next to me. His hand settles over his belly and his curled body hair moves every time he exhales and says, "Wow that was just great." At that instant, all I want to do is shake his shoulders and say, "That was just sex, David. We had sex. Move on. Move on." To distract myself, I count in my head. *One, two, three...*

Several pairs of footsteps thump on the carpet outside past our door. Perhaps girls in tight and bright clothes, accompanying balding, married men while the planet scurries indifferently. I blink my eyes several times, as people do when they sense a change in light.

"So you go to college or something?" He looks at me, narrowing his eyes.

"Yeah, Fine Arts." I look at my chipped toenail.

He turns towards me with a nameless urgency.

"This semester is about Renaissance music." I pull the covers up to my chin.

"Who is your favorite, kid," he asks, moving closer. "Mozart, Beethoven?"

"Bach."

"Bach, eh? He was my favorite too, the best organist. Even Mozart and Beethoven recognized his work, though it was before their time and very different." He sits up startled by his excitement.

"What did you say you do?" I try to get rid of the image of his thrusting, slim butt between my legs.

"Accounting." He gives a defeated look. "But I have always loved classical music... Anyway, you ..."

His cell vibrates. "Yes, honey, I should be home by dinnertime, how are the boys...?" His voice drifts into a careful whisper as he closes the bathroom door.

I hear the ticking clock, the slow thuds behind the walls as if something is moving. I slide my gaze across the room. Outside, the rain comes down pushing through open, flat land and single storied rooftops of deserted offices, smashing against the closed window. Concentric circles of heat and wind bring a sick sensation in my stomach. It's a profoundly familiar, criminal feeling. I start counting and place my hands over my breasts, massaging and collecting them. Feels like they'd hurt if I do not hold them.

"Love you," he says into his phone as he appears.

I lay there, feeling my breath rise through my limp body, subtly reminding me what I need to do next.

"So, do you play any instrument?"

"Trumpet."

"That mouth, I should have guessed." He pauses to register my expression. I get up.

"I'll take a nap before heading out. Feel free to stick around or whatever." He pulls out a moderate stack of twenties from his wallet.

"I'd like to shower before I go, if it's alright with you." I gather my clothes and take the money.

He nods and gives me a full look sliding his gaze over the curve of my hip and quickly recovering from it. "Trumpet, huh?" He keeps looking down at my lips as if he's reconstructing and rearranging them.

I smile with slight impatience.

"In three weeks?"

"Yeah, sounds good."

"Umm," he pauses as he looks down, pushing his big toe into the carpet as if he is about to make a strange declaration. "You don't have to do this. I mean, I like it. I like it very much. But I'd also like to talk to you. About music. Maybe we can talk more next time." His lips tremble into a delicate silence as he moves his hands over his head making sure I understood what he just said.

"Yeah," I say, my voice wrinkled with uncertainty as I open and close the bathroom door. I hear an airplane coming to land. I imagine the passengers looking outside the window, relieved to see the ground so close after hours of flying. I also assume what might happen after three weeks—fucking on the windowsill and on the bed and up against the wall. Making a lot of noise, deaf to the sound of take offs and landings, the thumping of steps outside—growing detachment. Or talking about music— oscillating between octaves of our likes and dislikes and leaving the room with a flat note in our voice. I look at my reflection. *She* is slowly settling under my skin like molten chocolate in a mold.

"Talking to you about music? What a load of horse shit," *she* says.

I try to break the spell, but *she* freezes a part of me. I can hear David snoring lightly. Holding tight, the roll of twenties in my fist, I feel like crying. From terror or guilt, or both. I think of my mother cooking dinner. I imagine walking in trying not to meet her eyes as she gives me a good-natured hug. Then she sips her beer and says, "Here's to a long day." And I agree. We eat dinner, kiss each other goodnight and fall asleep, waiting for the next day to be better than today. Still searching and wanting. Hoping to wake up with an answer, but losing it in the first hour of the day while looking for that one pair of socks that does not have holes yet.

Outside, the rain falls like soft feathers, with a wet hiss. I can smell another thunderstorm. The girl in the mirror is staring at me, making me feel like an outsider in my body. I exhale and close my eyes. Thoughts rush like blood gushing through every artery. Rental for the trumpet, a pair of snow boots, leather gloves? Maybe repair Mom's car. Or just save and watch it grow as if it were a living thing.

When I open my eyes, *she*'s gone but a layer of skin is crawling inside me, clotting my senses. I move my fingers on the neck and feel the flutter of my pulse. *One, two, three...*

Across the centuries, the rumbling calls out to her

Winds blow, brush past a bruise on Rama's upper arm. Three days ago, her husband pinched her skin with hot tongs because the chapatis she served him were cold. She presses the dark patch, imagines her husband shredding cane in a sugar factory not far from where she sells vegetables along with other greengrocers. His hands—rough like granular, tea-colored soil of the Deccan Plateau. A train whistles in the distance. Her toddler, nibbling on a baby carrot next to the wicker basket, pauses. She mouths *chook-chook* and sways her upper body. The toddler grins, slivers of carrot stuck near his lips.

*

In the tenth century, Rama is part of the Indian Deccan trap rock—her bosom holds hills, her midriff is invaded with rivers that swell during the monsoon, merge into the sea in weird positions.

*

To distract herself from the unbearable heat, Rama closes her eyes and counts all the lakes in the city. She feels tired, a thousand years old. Beads of sweat everywhere. She runs her fingers on her face as if tracing a map, finding clues of places and people she came from. A pointed nose and a small chin, a wide, remarkable forehead. The toddler is asleep. Flies circle over his head. When she opens her eyes, the sun is high up, making the crooked skyline of the city sparkle.

*

Rama is a mermaid in the Arabian Sea in the thirteenth century; her head resembles a cobra. She swims in the dark waters, entwines a giant rock until her hard scales slowly smooth it into a mirror. She decomposes staring at her reflection.

*

Rama fans away flies, adjusts her baskets and calls out to customers. The toddler crawls around, picks up dirt. Two women at a fruit stall next to the grocers are discussing the best days to visit the cliffs topped with deities and shrines. The ground shudders under Rama's feet when a train goes by. Sometimes it's the same rumbling she hears inside her sleep, calling out to her.

*

In the early fifteenth century, Rama is a tribal princess in eastern India, her face luminous, her hair set in tight curls, all set to bear a strong heir. She nurtures the lush folds of her belly and walks slowly to balance her weight, her golden chains dangling between her bare breasts, her skin dark, rich. She chooses a mate, delivers a girl. The girl possesses a rare beauty that drives men mad.

*

The day stretches like a long dream and the greengrocers slide their *pallus*, exposing their cleavage and arms. Male hawkers pass by, singing Bollywood songs. The women laugh and curse as they adjust the pleats of their sarees, a tickle of desire in their bellies. Afterwards, they sit and wait, their temples dripping with sweat.

The early dusk sky is crimson. Rama arranges the leftovers, picks up her toddler while another grocer helps with placing the basket on Rama's head. She thinks of the man who squeezed her hand while handing her change. The unmistakable lust in his eyes and how for a moment Rama wanted him to kiss her sunburned neck.

*

Four centuries ago, Rama is a courtesan. Her eyes heavily lidded—two moons rising out of the clouds. *Nawabs* and princes visit her *Kothi* to learn etiquette, understand music until she falls in love with one of her pupils, a boy with long lashes and pink privates. After he marries a princess from a neighboring province, Rama gives up her profession, lives inside a cave in a mountain, her robes riddled by moths, ants marching on her limbs. The earth licks her skin, makes her grow roots.

*

After folding the laundry, Rama whips three eggs in a bowl and lights the stove. When the toddler cries, she holds him just above her hip. A thought creeps in of leaving her husband tonight. Her toes press the unswept floor. The next moment, she imagines biting his earlobes, arching her torso, letting him splash her insides white, as if that's the natural course of her feelings. She watches the red-yellow oil, separating from the spices yet a part of it. Like land and water crisscrossing for centuries, touching the sky and falling, bodies slowly invading another, each time accessing a depth full of hunger, ungauged, unseen.

Spawn

I have a bunny in my stroller, nibbling on twigs and sprouts. Its claws tap my cell phone screen and call my contacts. Then, overcome with amazement, it pulls the Velcro on the inside flap of the stroller, snuggles behind a baby blanket. I call him Brownie.

"How can you stand it?" my husband says, struck with logic, staring at Brownie's muddy fur pads. He suggests I should see a therapist. But what does he know? He hasn't felt the babies who have unfurled and fizzled inside me. He hasn't felt the sadness that grows month after month when the dark fluid stains my thighs, leaves outlines on my panties after countless wash cycles. I exhale deeply and take Brownie to the playground, watch children going up and down the slides, screeching in delight, hanging upside down on monkey bars like bats. When they fall, their mothers hug them, wipe their tears, brush the dirt off their knees. Brownie sits in my lap, placid and waiting, while I wave and smile. In response, a few women chomp their upper lips and walk away with their kids, their bodies becoming smaller, then impossible to see. Others sit on the bench, their shoulders hunched, gazing at the horizon clear coated with birdsong.

The next morning, I carry Brownie in a shoulder bag to a convenience store. It peeps from the open zipper of the bag, biting its teeth into the leather, its brown eyes contrasting with big, black pupils.

In the afternoon, we drive to the outskirts of our blue-collar town—past the railway tracks, surrounded by cornfields, growing and browning of stalks. We roll in loam and sickly yellowing Midwestern light as jet streams slash the sky and freighters honk on a single-lane highway that circles the county. Dogs howl in the distance, the air smells of roasted potatoes and dust. We lie face up, enthralled by a lone cloud—tranquil, unfazed by the rustle. At night, Brownie and I dig the ground in the backyard under a constant throbbing of stars. Feel the day's warmth in the lumps of dirt. After an hour, Brownie hops away but comes back, its fur against my skin, its heart beneath my palm while the darkness breathes perfect, round dew in our hair and eyelids. I sing a lullaby, the timbre of my voice ingrained in the flickering orange glow of the streetlight.

When the dawn froths, I make out my husband's profile in the doorway, a sweep of his hair. He holds my hand, takes me inside. Wipes my face and cleans the dirt under my nails, breathes deeply as if he's about to go under. "It can't go on," he says, his sudden, broken-glass voice. "Brownie can't call out loudly from a crib, Brownie can't suck your breasts." Before he leaves the room, I glance at the sweat on his brow, a bloodstain between the breadcrumbs on his shirt. Misty-eyed, I stare outside the window to a mound of soil circled by golden light. And I want to hold Brownie, cling to it like a fish, kiss its ears. "Brownie," I howl, the sound sharp like its teeth. Everything stays still except a startled crow that swoops up in panic towards an unyielding, colorless sky.

Hum

The first time the tall girl brings a dwarf home, she's unsure. But the purpose is to get away from exotic, immaculate men and ordinary routine of sex and breakups. She is an executive in an ad agency, kohl-lined eyes and shoulder-length hair, has a taste for fancy things. Together, the girl and the dwarf walk hand in hand into her living room—bold and messy with high ceilings, heaps of leggings and flared tops on the leather couch, mismatched socks and size-nine shoes scattered on the hardwood floor.

The bed is too big for the dwarf, so the girl places pillows at the periphery. He talks dirty in his thick, deep voice, his tongue occasionally swirling along her neck, his head settled between her breasts like a new planet, listening to a humming inside her body, louder, ecstatic. She grows wet as he circles his middle finger around her navel; calls it the center of the universe. When he lifts his face to watch her, she gasps and pushes his head back, as if she is breathing through his mouth between her legs. She wakes up hungry—for him, for food.

The dwarf has ocean-sized, brown eyes. His disheveled hair makes him look like a ball of storm moving from one room to another. The girl tells him about her recent romances—men who complimented her athletic body, later complained about her long legs and short torso. Men, who straightened and winced, talked about sports, technology, politics, their voices hammer against steel. Men, who like sand, kept shifting under her shadow. The dwarf leans forward as he rubs oil on her back, his nose a massage stone, his prickly head a loofah. "All you need is a little unconditional love," he whispers, and climbs on her. They press their bodies—he tugs her earlobes, she pinches his nose, they sleep tangled up like necklaces in a jewelry box. In the following weeks, the girl's body grows and gleams; her skin bright and hypnotic, soaking sunrays, the humming inside her—a flap of butterfly wings.

Months fall and the girl delivers a star with a blazing tail, its edges sharper and brighter than anything she'd ever seen. Together, they plant it in their yard. The girl goes to work, and the dwarf sweeps the floor and scrubs the sinks, folds the laundry, waters the star.

Over years more stars are born, all rooted outside, some die young from fast combustion, others shimmer with kindling warmth, tiny darts of lightning around them—a twenty-four-hour glow.

While they are happy in a dreamlike life, the girl realizes the dwarf has leaked into her—her hair wiry and unruly, her voice a deep rumble. He has faded—his clothes two sizes too big for him. A shudder runs the length of her enormous body. Catching her breath, she asks what's happening to them. "My love we're becoming one. Everything is connected to everything," the dwarf answers, his sound a miniscule noise. She smiles thinking he still has a way with words. Until she can't move and swoons in her bed all day, calling his name, a piercing sad hum picking up inside her. Now a wandering speck because he has nothing left to offer, the dwarf stands at her eyelash or hangs by the long nail of her index finger, holding up to the pull of life, trying to find meaning in their perfect companionship. Sometimes he lets go to float in the space, unleashed. Later, tired and bored, he curls inside the well of her naval or edges himself into her dimpled cheek—eyeing the glistening orbs outside, his heart a blank horizon—empty of stars.

A Surprising Frailty

(handwritten margin note: roll into night like a joint / poetry)

We roll into the night like a joint, high and yelling. We walk on across the asphalt, into the drumming rain. Ben has returned from Iraq. He still cuts himself, anxious when he'll be able to go back again. He tells us there is nothing there, just desert and darkness. Sometimes, I am unnerved by the way he moves his eyes, wide and narrow as if he can pick up my thoughts.

Bill follows me everywhere. I grow sore of his company because he is dumb morning, noon and evening, forever. But he is strong and runs like a horse. I envy his legs; want to replace mine with his if there is such a thing possible.

Elantra has blonde hair and small eyes. She is like a stick that can bend and hit but never break. In another life, she might *(handwritten margin note: reincarnation)* have been an assassin. She carries a knife inside her clothes and has spent a few nights in jail. Her eyes are always searching for more. We call her Mother.

There are days when we drive our dirt bikes and fall into swamps, swim in the nearest lake and lie naked on the shore. We dig up worms, arrange them on the sand as alphabets, sunlight pressing on them forming a message. Mother likes to swim and hold one of us underwater as long as she wants. Then she lets us fuck her.

On every other weekend, Mother arranges street fights, with members of other gangs. And before we know, one of us is knotted with a stranger, our eyes stinging with dirt, and our noses bleeding. Whether we win or lose, Mother takes us home, tends us from head to toe. She calls the fights lovemaking of a different kind that lets out our darkness. According to her, in the future we may not have bodies at all.

Ben is the strongest fighter. It was Mother's idea to enlist him in the Army. Ben was in love with Mother. Until he went away and came back as a ghost with scars all over his body. Mother says cutting helps with the recovery of the soul.

Mother takes us to a party. A big house with loud music and young men yelling, squirming and straining. Windows fogged over with breath and smoke. I walk away after a bit and Bill joins me after a few minutes. It is a relief to step into a calm landscape, though our ears are still ringing. We stroll in the gated community, race to the lake, cartwheel on a golf course and drive their carts. We pee in a rose garden and run back to the house pretending we were there all along. The lie gives a surreal quality to the atmosphere around us. We are tired, but it feels good to hear Mother's voice, see her in a pale light, drinking and laughing. In that moment, she isn't any less or more but has a surprising frailty.

Like the rest of us. And it feels like the end of our universe and its discovery as she leans against Ben who shares a cigarette with Bill and me. All of us crushing light and smoke beneath our feet, smiling and hurting somewhere as we ride out, beyond that cartoony midnight, beyond the world with scars and street fights, war and an endless desert.

Half-White, Half-Charred

In the distance, along the hazy horizon, you see a settlement. *That's where the tribals live*, your wife says and curls her fingers on your arm. Her hand smells of cleaning agents—she's a clean freak—rushes to shower and makes you change the sheets, after you make love to her. Every time. *The tribals kidnap children; steal husbands,* your wife whispers—her chin resting on your shoulder. This is your second marriage and you aren't sure if this'll work too. Maybe you misread everything. Took all that organized shit as a sign of something proper. In any case, she hasn't yet complained of lint-infested corners or dusty fan blades and you haven't yet found an excuse to clear your throat to drown her words and walk away. You sip your tea, let the warmth stay in your mouth a bit longer than usual, and think of the tribal girl you saw standing on the roadside. Her bare toes digging the dirt, her big forehead marked by sparkling dots, her dark curls escaping from the bun like baby snakes emerging from a hole.

When your wife is away, surfing off the coast of Andaman, she sends text messages to you. *Miss you, Sweetie,* followed by a sparkling, throbbing heart emoji. Your fingers fumble over the text and then close the app. Outside the window, the overgrown grass sways in full sun. You decide to visit the settlement the next day, look for the girl. In the thin strains of dawn, the smoke billows up from a circle of tents. A woman, dressed in black, is about to duck into one of the canvas structures. *Hey,* you call out, and she turns around, her kohl-rimmed eyes, little moons. You follow her into the dwelling with a wispy peach curtain. Inside, it feels as if you've entered another universe— broken dolls and ripped scarves, sea-shell necklaces, metal bangles and anklets on the scattered pieces of rugs. She points you to a wooden stool and asks you to remove your wedding ring, your wristwatch. Then she sits across from you, pulls out a deck of cards. You open your mouth to say you aren't here for a tarot reading. Instead, you exhale and stare at her, completely still.

A few minutes later, the girl walks in—a raised pink in her cheeks and her neck, her gaze slippery. Maybe she saw you walking into the tent. You get up with a strong urge to touch her and she approaches you, a sly smile. Her fingers are dusted with soot, her chin tiny. She comes close, you can feel her breath on your nose: the loamy air that has left her and now wants to enter you. It's still so early in the day and there is a violent flutter in your stomach as she places her hand on your crotch. Gaseous and explosive. You allow her to unbutton your khakis, push you towards the floor, her skirt hitched up, her tan, tattooed legs straddling your pelvis. You bring your lips closer to the girl's mouth—it feels like the edge of a waterfall. The old woman shuffles the cards and starts cursing, her sharp voice dissecting the humidity. The curtain sways in a mild breeze and from the opening you catch a glimpse of a dipping clothesline touching the monsoon slick earth, the simmering coals on an angithi cooking a bird—its feathers half-white, half-charred. And you continue to slow dance inside the girl, still trying to believe that this is happening—your hand moving away from the girl's hips to her shoulders, reaching out to the dirty tassels of a nearby lamp, your palms laced in a shimmering cobweb, finding comfort. The air roils white. The dust rushes and settles on your skin, as if it has been waiting.

Separation

[handwritten annotations: "rhythm / poetry" and "deaf people"]

You never see the people because they keep different hours, but when the air conditioning isn't humming or the dishwasher isn't running, you hear what drops on the other side of the wall: books, silverware, curses translating into nightfall. The toilet flush followed by a shower. Every Friday evening, laughter, throbbing, pulsing of a body ruined by pleasure, receding click-clack of stilettos, the sealing sound of a shutting door. The vibration of the elevator. You wonder where they are going. Do they ever hear you? Some days you wait for a sound because you haven't spoken since the last conversation you had in your office before the weekend. The silence splits your brain. You press your ears harder to open them up. The teeth-white walls, the concrete floor below you, slightly uneven. Clap, thump of your slippers. You open the window, a bright summer haze falls on your clothes and your poetry books, on your face, squinting your eyes. Heat ripples in the air, settling a verse on your chapped lips. In the distance, a bulldozer demolishes an old building, an orange cloud growing around it. At first, the noise seems to be harsh and then a monastic chant, leveling the voices from another year, another decade, another century. You try to imagine their faces, emboldened jaws, sharp noses, expressive, bright eyes, perhaps, like the neighbors you have never met. The shining dust from the rubble streams in and mixes with your breath. Like a fish swimming to the surface for oxygen, you open your mouth wide, eat the day slowly.

Seams

We sleep in a room filled with mirrors. When the dawn breaks, I carve my baby out—same prism of nose, a pink mouth. Run my fingers through his hair gelled with mucus. Come nighttime, when moonlight streaks our bodies like paint, he snuggles back into my womb, mixes up his features. The mirrors hold his last image, help me fix him again.

The baby carries a silver seam ripper—making small incisions, plucking the edges of my body like a dress, when he comes out. His face is a smooth canvas. I shape the eyes, measure the distance between his chin and lips. I breathe into his mouth— pull out the ghosts of past lives.

I teach my baby how to walk barefoot, so everyone can see he has no secrets. I place his fingers on a piano. Play a full octave. The baby coos—matches his sounds to the music. Then he giggles and pushes his pink toes into my mouth. I want to bite, swallow him whole.

Frequently, while nursing, the baby stares at me, as if he knows what motherhood is. I sing a lullaby while we look outside, trees leaning against the mirror-room window, pigeons bobbing on their branches.

A glass echo of green. Tricky reflections—watching, seizing, letting go. The mirrors around us show the edges of my stomach, the white of my bones, our drifting moods. I tell my baby he's the only one who has broken my seams. He has made me bleed a river. He has let out the nightingales. He has let the wind in. I wonder who will love me now that my belly is stretched with fat, birthing seams. Who will want me since I can no longer disrobe shy or wear white? If anyone will give him chances to start over like I do. If anyone will like our chaos—the stains on our shirts, the scent of our tongues. The fact we're both failures—our senses only trained for each other, aching to understand. Only our love is real because we have carried it, felt its slop against our hips, hurt our backs holding it. Only we know it'll never be enough.

Enfold

After his death, my husband lives in the walls and fixtures of our home. They rumble and shake when he's pacing inside them, bulge and contract. Sometimes, an outline of a face emerges out of the paint. I blink hard, and it's gone.

My husband loved our home, the soft paneling, the silk lanterns, high ceilings, low wooden sofas, and our king-size four-poster bed. The French windows, a green echo of trees outside.

In the beginning I didn't know he was there. I mean there wasn't much to do before and after work, except to sleep, eat and stare at nothing, or fall asleep while watching the TV, holding the remote as if it was his hand. Until one day, while taking a shower, I looked at the vent and felt a rush of his breath on my face, a familiar cocktail of smells—Old Spice mixed with Listerine. He felt so near, and I stood naked, long after I'd finished, covered in goose bumps, trying to enfold my body in his scent.

In the dim lit evenings, when I return from work, our home looks dark and deserted, but I know that he's inside, sliding in the pipes, or crouched behind the toilet, or waiting in the closet. Often, I rest my head against the wall and sense his fingers in my hair, easing the day. A door hatch inside me opens. I let him in. Together we watch porn, try out different poses that I wasn't comfortable doing when he was alive. Afterwards, the bed gently rocks me to sleep, stacks my dreams on the side table, next to a broken clock and a dusty statue of a laughing Buddha.

For months we go on. I stop going to work. Dirty laundry piles up on the floor, unread mail stacks up on the kitchen counter. My head feels fuzzy. Something pulses between my legs desperately, constantly. I hear his heartbeat beneath the ground, deep and low. "You're dead," I say out loud one day, I write it down a hundred times. Then I load the laundry, pour chemicals on the floor, the scent of polish fills my head. The task of waxing and buffing makes me forget.

When I finish and walk outside, the sky is the color of a tinted church window. From the driveway, our home hunches like an old man—a stone exterior on the front, vinyl sidings, and a sick yellow inside the lamps. The kitchen garden is a swamp, the rose bush is dead. It has rained recently, the mud caking around my feet, more and more with each step.

In the backyard, hangs a birdhouse, there's shit all over it. Birds come in and go. A lumpy silhouette of a forgotten grill, a picnic table that needs a fresh coat of paint. Whispery glints of fallen leaves. I sit on the patio floor. The concrete is hard and cold. I am on my hands and knees—my body low on the ground like a strange, ancient creature, listening to the low vibration of him— muffled words admitting his want, my restraint falling away like daylight—and then only stars, a heat of blush traveling up my neck, the fabric of his breath shaped around me like a shimmering gown.

Shedding

In a neighboring slum in Mumbai, the open stage is flooded with blue and green strobes. Rockstar Sweetie's dazzling—tight golden pants and a matching unbuttoned jacket. Goggles and metallic chains. He calls Ajmera, my stepmother, on stage and together they hip-hop on Bollywood duets. Ajmera stumbles in her high heels and Sweetie seizes her arm, keeps her upright. The rest of us sway like a slow night.

Ajmera is a thirtysomething homebody living with me after my father died. But here she's radiant in a silver skirt and a busty green top—shimmies with Sweetie as if she's a teenager like me and has never been touched.

Sweetie stays over for chicken curry and peppered rice, Ajmera's specialty. His eyes, brown and shrunk, blink hard. There's something girlish about his hair, long with bangs. Later, I wake up in the living room—dark and hot. When I walk outside, I can see through the bedroom's open window. Ajmera's naked, her legs wrapped around Sweetie. A flickering streetlight makes them appear and disappear. Lunge and hide.

*

Weeks later, I see an egg in the bedroom—oblong, off-white.

"We need to throw it somewhere far away from here." Ajmera stands next to me and presses the heel of her palms to her eyes. Blood trickles down her thighs. I open my mouth, but words get lost—part fear, part disgust. That evening we walk silently past the railway tracks, past the sugar factory, leave the egg under a Banyan tree.

*

The next time, Sweetie stays for a whole month, inserts himself into our lives. He gets flowers and cosmetics for Ajmera, calls her Darling. I feel aroused and irritated as if those feelings are supposed to belong together.

At night I imagine Sweetie's cool touch beating the stuffy humidity of the city and my body, dream about a heap of eggs on the outskirts of Mumbai, released into the sea: half-snake, half-human clones of Sweetie swimming back to the shore, winking at me.

*

Ajmera delivers another egg; her skin looks pale and wrung out, the white of her eyes shot through with tiny red veins.

"He's cursed," I warn her.

She smirks, her hands covered in soap foam, the water from the tap splashing from the surface of a dirty dish.

"You want him, don't you?" She glances at me as we're walking towards the banyan. "That forked tongue in your mouth, those slippery scales between your legs. A brand-new body that emerges after shedding. O' so sweet."

*

The next few times when Sweetie's around, I borrow backless blouses with miniskirts from my friends, wear low-cut tops and fitted jeans. Every time he kisses Ajmera, the heaviness in my chest grows; my eyes water.

One evening when Ajmera's outside, Sweetie sits next to me while I'm watching TV and places his hand on my thigh. I go slippery inside. "You know what I'd like to do to you?" He removes his glasses, brings his face closer to mine. "I'd like to peel away that spotless skin of yours and wear it, so it never sheds again."

*

Ajmera feeds on her eggs. Sweetie's recommendation. She looks slender, her face glows. And all I think is if Sweetie would have me once she's gone. One late morning, I walk into the bedroom, quiet as a secret. Sweetie's drunk from the previous night and snoring. Ajmera's next to him, her fingers laced in his. When I place the curved blade against her neck, she jerks and breathes hard. The meat knife drops and I see her face—afraid, familiar, and desperate to hold onto love. In a flash her body turns purple and then darker, narrows into a snake that slithers outside the window. Sweetie hisses, raises his hood. For the first time I see his body, like a long scar on a face, like a crack in the floor. "Wait," I say and start crying but he lowers himself and follows her. Outside, the birds go crazy as if they've spotted danger. I close the window and lean against the wall with a memory of their presence, just empty, missing. Under the hot air circulating from a ceiling fan, a snakeskin trembles on the bed.

ACKNOWLEDGEMENTS

For everyone in my family, especially my children and my husband who have made me a better person, my parents who have always encouraged me, my younger brother who has given voice to my childhood, and my in-laws who have accepted me with open arms and hearts. You're forever first. Love you always.

For the readers of my stories, their feedback, their kindness, and their constant support of my work.

For Sally Houtman, my mentor, my friend, who thought my voice was unique and powerful, who endlessly worked on the drafts of my earlier stories to make them perfect, who went away too soon. I miss you.

For Okay Donkey Press, for Eric Newman, and for Genevieve Kersten for believing in me and making this real.

Thank you.

Stories in this collection have appeared, sometimes in a slightly different form, in the following publications:

"Alligators" in *Barrelhouse*

"Lunar Love" in *Waxwing*

"Wherever, Whenever" in *Jet Fuel Review*

"Up and Up" in *The Arkansas International*

"Milk" in *The Minnesota Review*

"Scooped-Out Chest" in *TypeHouse*

"Spaceman" in *Third Point Press*

"Piecing" in *TriQuarterly*

"Silent Spaces" in *Emry's*

"the shrinking circle" in *Isthmus*

"Girl Loss" in *Pithead Chapel*

"In Its Entire Splendor" in *Vestal Review*

"The Moons of Jupiter" in *Rappahannock Review*

"Cubes" in *Wigleaf*

"Mumtaz in Burhanpur" in *Bat City Review*

"We're Waiting to Hear Our Names" in *Mojo, Mikrokosmos*

"New Old" in *The Southampton Review*

"Nine Openings" in *Squalorly*

"Poison Damsels in Rajaji's Harem, 1673" in *The Tishman Review*

"Whatever Remains" in *Tin House*

"Spin" in *The Cincinnati Review*

"A Thousand Eyes" in *PANK*

"The Fortune Teller" in *Barren Magazine*

"Snowstorm" in *Atticus Review*

"Uncouple" in *The Arkansas International*

"Only Buildings" in *Paper Darts*

"Acid of Curiosity" in *Parcel*

"Subsong" in *The Mondegreen*

"Ghosht Korma" in *SmokeLong Quarterly*

"The Undecided Colors" in *Lost Balloon*

"Hands" in *The Sonder Review*

"Infinite" in *Juked*

"Measurable Hours" in *Literary Orphans*

"Bikini Wax" in *Lunch Ticket*

"Feeding Time" in *OKAY Donkey*

"What Might Come After You" in *Rathalla Review*

"A Closed Circuit" in *Hot Metal Bridge*

"Between Not Much and Nothing" in *PidgeonHoles*

"Clueless" in *Yalobusha Review*

"Egress" in *2Bridges Review*

"Milk Chocolate Messenger Man" in *Carbon Culture*

"Across the centuries, the rumbling calls out to her" in *Duende*

"Spawn" in *Fiction International*

"Hum" in *New Flash Fiction Review*

"A Surprising Frailty" in *Whiskey Paper*

"Half-White, Half-Charred" in *Ghost Parachute*

"Separation" in *Gigantic Sequins*

"Seams" in *Mid-American Review*

"Enfold" in *The Citron Review*

"Shedding" in *Hot Metal Bridge*

Made in the USA
Coppell, TX
22 January 2021

48577204R00121